Also by Julian F. Thompson
TERRY AND THE PIRATES

HARD TIME

JULIAN F. THOMPSON

ATHENEUM BOOKS FOR YOUNG READERS
NEW YORK LONDON TORONTO SYDNEY SINGAPORE

Atheneum Books for Young Readers
An imprint of Simon & Schuster Children's Publishing Division
1230 Avenue of the Americas
New York, New York 10020
Book design by O'Lanso Gabbidon
The text of this book is set in Garamond.
Printed in the United States of America

2 4 6 8 10 9 7 5 3
Library of Congress Cataloging-in-Publication Data
Thompson, Julian F.
Hard time / Julian F. Thompson.—1st ed.
p.   cm.
Summary: When a district attorney who is eager to make an
example of a teenaged offender misinterprets an essay written by
fifteen-year-old Annie Ireland, Annie, her best friend Roach Boy,
and Primo, a magical being who is trapped in a doll's body, are sent
first to jail then to a cross between a school and boot camp.
ISBN: 0-689-85424-2 (hardcover)
[1. Justice, Administration of—Fiction. 2. Magic—Fiction.
3. Dolls—Fiction. 4. Schools—Fiction. 5. Reformatories—
Fiction. 6. Interpersonal relations—Fiction.] I. Title.
PZ7.T371596 Har 2003
[Fic]—dc21   2003005157

For Polly and her hench-dog, Reggie, who've sentenced me to easy, happy time

1.

The Baby

"When we're born," Annie Ireland told the Roach Boy once, "we're sentenced to, like, *life*. And some of us—I'd be a prime example—are made to do hard time."

She didn't blame that solely on the baby, though.

The baby, or "your baby," as Ms. Beach referred to it when she handed Annie hers, was a life-size doll. All the freshman girls at Converse High who were enrolled in the required Life Skills class were given their own babies to take care of. So Annie had to have the baby with her all day, every school day. Wherever she was, she bottle-fed it, burped it, and changed it, according to Ms. Beach's schedule. It slept through most of Annie's classes, though, a sign of its intelligence, she thought. The baby was an anatomically correct boy who had "nothing to write home about," according to Laird Sediment, a guy in Annie's class who liked to watch and snicker during diaperings.

Annie didn't think she needed Life Skills class. She didn't need to be warned about what would happen if she played unprotected hide the weenie with the Roach Boy, the only male with whom she had had so much as *social* intercourse. And she didn't have to learn "responsibility." Shit, she thought, if anything, she was *too* responsible already, too perennially conscience-stricken and turning cartwheels to do better, to live up to her parents' endless row of "We expect's."

Ann Ireland

Other than her parents, people called Ann Ireland "Annie" as a rule, because she looked more like an Annie. Annies are a little wide-eyed and have energy to burn. They can, and this one did, have freckles. She called her freckles "brain spots," though, and claimed they were caused, not by the sun, but by intelligent energy erupting out of the top of her head showering her face. The zits that occasionally appeared on her forehead and chin, however, were almost certainly the result, she believed, of eighteen-wheelers full of both anxiety and stress that were driven into her psyche by her parents, emptied of their cargoes, and then abandoned with their motors running.

Annie wasn't captivated by her face. She'd seen worse, but also much, much better. To begin with, this physiognomy of hers decorated the front of a head that was shaped like a honeydew melon, and it was therefore much too much like the heads of the kids in the Peanuts comic strip. Her small nose was a little punky, she thought, and that was good. When she wrinkled it (like, in disgust), her face had "attitude." But her size XL mouth and big brown eyes weren't team players. If she forgot to keep them under strict control, they were much too quick to widen (yes, excitedly, enthusiastically) and so become "cheerleaderish." *That* wasn't good at all.

"For heaven's sake, try not to leave the house looking so *plain*," Annie's mother had been known to say. And then she might tack on, "I can't imagine where this *limp* hair comes from," while flicking up the ends of her daughter's light brown, totally straight, and not-at-all-thick ponytail. "It's not what you'd expect to find on someone with your father's genes, and mine." Annie had tried the extra-body shampoo she'd seen advertised on TV, but still her hair refused to move seductively, and massively, and glowingly, even when she'd blow-dried it, and brushed it till her arm ached, and swung her head (like on TV) from side to side.

Her body didn't cheer her up a whole lot either. In some of her clothes, including the baggy overalls she often wore to school, she appeared to be flat-chested, even though she wasn't, totally. And it seemed unfair to her that someone who'd been given small boobs, like herself, would get a pair that weren't a perfect match. But at least she didn't have to put up with the disgustograms that followed girls with D-cups down the halls of learning. And only the few people who'd seen her in a swimsuit knew that she had nicely sculpted calves and thighs. These were not, she claimed, inherited, but came from all the running up and down the stairs she'd done—for years and years—while trying to "be an angel" and retrieve whatever thing it was her father and her mother wanted her to bring them from their bedroom, their bathroom, or the attic.

Annie was afraid that, overall, she looked tomboyish. And it seemed her father might feel the same. "No woman is Ann Ireland," he told her with a jolly smile; he'd just given her the once-over. "If I may take a liberty or two with old John Donne."

That little offhand insult stayed with her for years, even though she didn't "get" it till her summer reading list included *For Whom the Bell Tolls*.

3.

The Fire

There were several possible explanations for how the fire started.

Maybe it was because Annie's mother forgot she'd put a lamb chop in the Gorge Foreman Lean, Mean, Fat-Reducing Grilling Machine before she went upstairs to bed.

Or it might have been because her husband, Annie's father, had been shooting at the pigeons who were based at an out-of-town farm but who'd come and landed on a window ledge outside their bedroom. What he liked to do was fill a water pistol with cigarette lighter fluid and shoot it through a lighted match. This turned the pistol into a miniature flamethrower. It's possible a misdirected salvo set the bedroom drapes on fire.

And, of course, it could have been a lightning strike, or faulty wiring, or a pile of oily rags spontaneously combusting in the basement. Those were the most likely causes, according to Hieronymus "Happy" Holliday, the chief of the Converse

Volunteer Fire Department. "One of them three's gotta be the one," he said. "No doot aboot it."

Whatever its cause, the fire had a good start before anyone became aware of it. Annie might not have inherited her parents' hair, but she slept the same way they did: like a rock. It took some hollering before she came awake and got a whiff of smoke.

"Ann! ANN! Ann-EEEE!" was what she heard. "Do rouse yourself, for pity's sake. It seems these premises have caught on fire!"

"Huh? Wha-Wha-Wha? Say who?" said Annie, not all there yet. She staggered out of bed. She first believed that the hollerer was her dear daddy-o and that this was just another of his lame attempts at humor. But when she opened her bedroom door, with resentment bubbling upward from her heart, and stuck her head into the hall, she could see there wasn't anybody there. What *was* there, instead, was smoke, quite a bit of smoke, along with crackling sounds and heat more site-specific than, say, global warming.

She quickly shut the door again, now wide awake.

"The window," said the same voice. It was coming from *inside* the room, not from the hall. It was a man's voice, a strange man's voice. It sounded sort of wonky, like on PBS.

"I rather think it's time we make our exit through the window," it went on. "From out there on the porch roof it's a short drop to the ground—no danger to a young and healthy woman like yourself. Though I'd suggest you bend your knees and so absorb a little of the shock of landing, if you'd be so kind. That should save some wear and tear on both us."

Annie turned on her bedroom light. The voice had seemed to come from way across the room. Maybe from her closet. Perhaps a homeless man had come and taken refuge there, the afternoon before, while she was still at school. And only now was he waking from an alcoholic stupor.

So, she addressed the closet door.

"Who's there?" she said. "Who's in my closet?"

But there wasn't any answer.

Between her and the closet was a fat, upholstered chair on which sat the baby. Its baby blues were fixed on her, and she thought its lips had narrowed, tightened, as if it were impatient or annoyed.

"Come on," said Annie, out loud but to herself. "It can't have been the baby."

"Maybe not *the baby* . . . ," said the same voice, now sarcastically.

Annie rubbed her eyes. Now it seemed to her the baby's lips were moving.

"The speaker," said the baby, "is, indeed, myself. Pantagruel Primo, Esquire, at—as I certainly hope you'll come to realize, fast—your service." He pronounced his last name "Preemo."

There was now no doubt that the doll was speaking. As well as looking somewhat older. A cigar would not have seemed completely out of place, had there been one in the corner of his mouth. He was very nearly bald, and Annie thought that short, bald men were apt to smoke cigars.

"I'm dreaming," Annie said. "Or I've gone nuts. The Roach

Boy said he thought we might. He said that trying to cope with being teenage in a new millennium could drive us mad."

"Luckily for us both," said Pantagruel Primo, Esquire, "you're neither dozing nor demented. So perhaps you'll put your fundament in gear and get us out of here? Before we're victims of a premature cremation? Before our real identities are ascertainable only by means of dental records?"

"Okay," said Annie, nodding hard, now accepting her own wakefulness and sanity, now focused on the fact that the house, her house, was taking step one on the way to becoming a smoldering ruin. "Gimme just a sec to see what I should try to save."

Deciding wasn't easy. Even though she'd have a nonpareil excuse, she'd done the written homework for the next day the afternoon before, so she thought it'd be a waste to leave it to the flames. So that was the first thing she packed. And she realized she could save some space in her backpack if she got out of her pj's and into real clothes, so she did that before it even occurred to her that Pantagruel Primo, Esquire, was sitting there watching the whole time. She grabbed some necessary makeup and a handful of necklaces and earrings off her dressing table. Then she stuffed in her ancient teddy bear, Neddy, who was born, her mom had said, just a year after Annie herself. And she stuck on her favorite baseball cap—the one with MELIOR FORTUNA-TEM QUA BONUM on the front of it, which meant (according to the Roach Boy) "I'd rather be lucky than good"—and pulled her ponytail through the hole in the back of it.

Finally, for reasons of diplomacy, she plucked the photo of her parents off the wall, and then the fake ID from her underwear drawer, because it'd be just her luck to have the good-hands guy from Allstate find it, once the fire was put out.

Of course, the last thing she picked up to save was Pantagruel Primo, Esquire, aka (to everyone but her) "her baby."

The next week's issue of the *Converse Tribune* made much of that heroic act, describing it as "an untainted flowering of pure maternal instinct."

Annie's parents left the burning house about the same time she did, carrying two large suitcases stuffed with checkbooks, jewelry, and resort wear, down the fire escape that was accessible from (just) their dressing room.

4.

The Roach Boy

Arby, the famous Roach Boy, didn't physically resemble either kind of roach. He wasn't flat or loathsome, on the one hand. Nor was he stubby, burned out, and rich in tetrahydrocannabinol, on the other. In the "looking" department he was somewhere between average- and funny-. His ears stuck out a bit, and his Adam's apple was larger than most people's. His hair was the same unremarkable brown as Annie's, but it was wavier, cut short, and parted on one side. He had a good-size nose that tilted up a little, and his chin receded slightly, giving him (Annie thought) a good face for walking into the wind. Annie loved his eyes. They were huge and had long lashes. She'd heard that someone's eyes were the windows of that person's soul. Looking into the Roach Boy's, she saw pure truthfulness and sweetness. He was slender, five foot nine and still shooting up, and cut high, with long legs and big floppy feet.

The boy had an unfortunate first and last name. It was Nemo Skank, a name that's easy to make fun of, the sort of name that little kids can chant and rhyme with "toilet tank." So Annie took his Roach Boy initials, R. B., and called him "Arby"—"Ar" or "Arb," for short.

Anyway, the reason he was famous was that every weekend, from the middle of September to the middle of November, he lay in the dimness of a glass-sided box in a Halloween-centered amusement park called the Fright Factory. There, wearing a short-sleeved and above-the-knee-length wet suit with a hood, along with a snorkeler's face mask, he allowed himself to be turned into a human serving platter for who-knows-how-many hungry cockroaches. They swarmed all over his body as he lay there, scarfing down the stuff that Fright Factory employees had smeared on him, which a sign announced was GENUINE UNDER-THE-REFRIGERATOR gunk. A bright light controlled by a timer would go on inside the box every five minutes, and as if by magic, all the roaches would disappear. The public loved that feature; it provoked a lot of "Ooh's" and "Ah's" and "Wow's" and "Look at that's."

Kids often asked the Roach Boy how he got the job and what it felt like to have disgusting-looking insects scurrying around on his body, often on bare skin, sometimes even ducking down between his toes.

He said he guessed he got the job the same way everybody gets jobs: by being in the right place at the right time. What he didn't say (except to Annie) was that the place was his uncle's kitchen, the uncle who was the "silent partner" in the Fright Factory's ownership, at the moment when the uncle said, "Hey,

Nemo, howja like to make twenny bucks an hour, weekends, widout havin' to lift a finguh?"

And he said he hardly felt the bugs at all.

"They're awfully light," he'd tell whoever asked. "They never bite or anything. And 'cause I have that suit and hood and mask on, they can't crawl into any of my . . . orifices."

The Roach Boy was on display in the box for four hours at a time, from 1:30 to 5:30 P.M., and then again from 6:30 to 10:30. Between 5:30 and 6:30, he went home, took a shower, put on a fresh wet suit, ate, came back to the Fright Factory, and got regunked for the second show.

"If dinner's something like spaghetti, I'm apt to be a pretty sloppy eater," he told Annie this one time, "but the nights I'm working, Mom doesn't rag on me about my table manners, like talking with my mouth full. She thinks the roaches like it if I've slopped a little something down my front. 'That'll be a nice change for them from the same old gunk,' she says."

Spending those eight hours in the box gave the Roach Boy lots of time to think. He devoted much of it to a simpleminded game that he thought up and called "What if . . . ?"

In it he asked himself such questions as, *What if, instead of being a little Honda, our family car was a tank, and I could drive it?* or *What if we were playing basketball in gym, and I had four long arms?* or *What if I put the keyboard of my word processor on the floor of my sister's hamster cage, and they printed out a ton of nonsense and one copy of each of my final exams?* In answering those questions, he'd imagine a lot of different outcomes that'd have one thing in common: He, the hero in each one, would have a ball.

But certain kinds of "What if . . . ?" questions were . . . unsuitable for use inside a glass-sided box while under public scrutiny, he quickly learned. *What if Cameron Diaz and I were shipwrecked on a desert island?* would be one such question.

The day after the fire Annie didn't get to school until after lunch. The Roach Boy and everybody else had learned by then that what was once her house, a charming center-hall colonial, was now a blackened shell. For more than fifteen minutes after her arrival Annie was the center of attention, and the Roach Boy didn't get a chance to really talk to her until the school day ended and the rest of the students were all talking about the cherry bomb in the boys' room toilet. Arby was relieved to see that after all that she'd been through, she still looked the same, with the same old backpack on her back and the same old baby in her arms.

"But what are you going to *do*?" he asked her. "You got a place to *live*?"

"Unfortunately, yes," said Annie. "I now have an enormous room in the Sachs mansion—you know, my uncle Orel and aunt Bunny's place, that big white elephant up on the hill. That means, of course, I'll also be cohabiting with Cousin Fleur."

"Oof," the Roach Boy said, and, "Bummer. But how come your folks decided to stay with the Sachses? I thought your mom despised her sister."

"Oh, yeah, she does," said Annie. "She wouldn't think of staying there herself. What's happened is that she and Pop have gotten deeply philosophical all of a sudden. They now believe that everything happens for a reason. Pretty deep stuff, huh? And that the reason for the fire was to . . . well, *uproot* them from their comfortable and self-indulgent day-to-day existence. They feel that they're now meant to bite the bullet and make a real commitment to a worthwhile cause."

"Which is?" the Roach Boy asked.

"Serious weight loss," Annie told him. "By them both."

"What?" the Roach Boy said. "That's why your parents think the fire happened—to get them to lose weight?"

"Yep," said Annie. "And they've already decided where to go to do that. It's a fat farm called Negative Feedback, way out in Arizona, or New Mexico, or maybe southern California, I'm not sure. Pop says it costs an arm and a leg, but it's worth it. There's a flat weekly rate, and then, on top of that, you pay them by the pound! The more weight you lose, the more you pay them. It's some version of reverse psychology, apparently, and paying lots and lots of money is like a prestige thing. Their motto is 'Let us do liposuction on your assets.' Mom said some Hollywood mogul coughed up two and a half million for a six-week stay. That's supposedly the record."

The Roach Boy shook his head. "But you—poor you—you'll meanwhile be going one-on-three with the Sachses all the time they're out there."

"Well, not exactly," Annie told him. "I'll have *him* with

me." And she nodded at the baby lying in her arms with his eyes closed.

The Roach Boy didn't seem impressed. "And you can always call *me* any night you need to talk," he said.

Annie decided then that she'd just tell him. She needed to tell *someone*, and Arby was the only someone in her life who wouldn't either laugh or try to cart her to the nearest psychiatric center.

"Don't laugh," she said, wanting to make sure he wouldn't, "but it turns out *he* can talk." She nodded at the baby once again. "Looks can be deceiving, Arb. Say hello to Pantagruel Primo, Esquire. You can call him by his last name or, if you'd rather, just by his initials."

Arby gave his friend a real close look and so became 99.9 percent convinced she wasn't kidding. It appeared to him that she was counting on him, even.

"Hello, P. P.," he said, a little slowly, cautiously. There was that tiny possibility that this was one of Annie's little jokes and that she was getting set to bust out laughing.

"Greetings and salutations, my young friend," said Pantagruel Primo, Esquire, his eyes snapping open. "You've been taken by surprise, of course. One doesn't as a rule encounter baby dolls inhabited by beings who have more to say than 'goo-goo-ga-ga' or a postprandial brr-ELCH!"

The Roach Boy had to smile. This Primo guy apparently possessed a skill he'd tried to master—unsuccessfully—for years: loud burping on demand. But still . . . How could a doll, like, *talk*?

"As I've explained to Annie," P. P., Esquire, went on, "many years ago, in places such as Iceland, Ireland, and some others, goblins, elves, and leprechauns, as well as other special beings large and small, were much more common than they are here in the USA today. Many spells were cast, for fun and profit, on humans in all walks of life: knights and queens and clergymen, adventurers and housewives and the working poor, not to mention the odd dragon. Grand times were had by all of us. But in this country, recently—regrettably, I'd say—we've lost our sense of mission and started arguing among ourselves. Little competitions have sprung up. We've started doing . . . things to one another, trying to prove who's cleverest and best." With that, he sighed and shook his head, and maybe even blushed.

"I've gotten shamefully, if cleverly, involved in that," Primo admitted with another sigh, but also just a smidgen of a smile. "I turned a troll name Slurpagar the Quaint into a toad with no stickum on its tongue on the day of the annual mayfly hatch." Then, apparently, he couldn't help himself: He chuckled. "You should have seen him firing blanks as many hundred helpings of his favorite food flew by. But of course that meant he owed me big time. I rather think he overdid it, but in any case, he fixed it so that I'm trapped here in this bogus baby body, able to move nothing but my head—including eyes and nose and mouth, of course. And here I'll stay for days, or weeks, or months—who knows how long? Only Slurpagar the Quaint, I guess. My plan, originally, was to not react at all to what he'd done to me—give him no reaction satisfaction. My intention was to wait him out in total silence."

"What made you change your mind?" the curious Arby asked.

"Two things," Primo told him. "The first was learning Annie is an Ireland. I assumed her father's people came from there originally. And me, I still have kinfolk on and under the Ould Sod. It's possible her folks and mine . . . interacted in some bygone day. I find I'm drawn to Annie Ireland." And he looked up at her and smiled.

"And then there came that unexpected and unwelcome happening," he continued. "That infernal fire. Had I not spoken— screamed my head off, almost—and waked Annie up, it's possible she would have passed out from the smoke, or even died. And if she'd only fainted and the firefighters broke in and hauled her out, I'd certainly have been left behind. Would I—the real me—have survived that holocaust? I just don't know. There's one thing I do know, though. What happened was that I saved her, then she saved me. Now I look upon the two of us as partners, beings with our fates entwined."

"D'you think there's any chance that someone *set* the fire?" Arby asked quite pointedly.

"Someone by the name of Slurpagar the Quaint? I don't think so," Primo answered, thinking: *Hey, this kid is sharp.* "We have rules against 'unnecessary roughness' in our dealings with one another.

Setting a fire might also be considered 'unsportsmanlike conduct.' Or 'illegal procedure,' at the very least."

"The firemen didn't think it was set," said Annie. "And, anyway, all that matters is that you're fine," she told her newfound friend.

"He thinks that he can still play tricks on people," she then said to Arby. "But he knows he can't cast off the spell he's under—this is in that rule book that he has to follow—and he also can't do anything, right now, to Slurpagar."

"But there are many worthwhile targets in your world," Primo told the boy. "Like, maybe on an outing one day soon we'll come upon a newly minted dot-com millionaire, just strutting down the street whilst talking on his cell phone. In that case, I might make a pair of long-haired dachshunds suddenly appear in front of him and have him first get tangled in their leashes, then trip and fall, landing on a slice of pizza or where a college student just threw up. That'd be a bit of fun, wouldn't you say?"

"Wow!" said Arby. "You could do a thing like that? How totally, completely neat!"

Although he'd never met an elf or gnome or troll before, he found it easy to believe that they existed and could do all sorts of far-out stuff. Being the Roach Boy had made him open to uncommon occupations. He supposed that if he were Irish or Icelandic, he would have come upon a lot of little people, but for a teenage resident of Converse, meeting someone like this guy P. P. (or Primo) had to be the thrill of his young lifetime.

And something that he hoped to take advantage of, or at least enjoy to the max. As his uncle liked to say, "Contacts make da woild go round."

"Meeting you is just an honor and a pleasure, sir," he continued, giving Primo his sincerest smile. "I hope I get to see you lots, before your spell gets broken and you . . . resume your real identity or whatever."

"There's no reason that you shouldn't," Primo said, "though how much we see each other will be mostly up to you. As you know, I am immobile, never far from Annie. Because you are a friend of hers and seem cut from the same good cloth, I welcome both your friendship and your company."

"Well, I'll try not to overdo it," Arby said. "I imagine that you like a little privacy at times. I mean, I know I wouldn't like to go back to being fed and burped and changed."

"Oh, the feeding and the burping parts don't bother me at all," P. P. replied. "They can be a welcome change from simply lying on my back and staring into space. But being changed is quite a different matter. Modesty is not the issue; I have none. And I don't mind Annie going through the motions; she has a schedule she has to follow at the pain of failure. I don't even care about her moronic classmate watching. What really, really rankles me, however, is knowing that, every time I'm changed, old Slurpagar is cracking up." He sighed. "Although I must admit I laughed until I damn near damped my breeches when he couldn't nab a single mayfly with that nonstick tongue of his."

5

At the Sachs House

Annie's uncle Orel was a balding, paunchy, red-faced man. Aunt Bunny had wrinkles and a perpetual tan, and she played a lot of tennis doubles with "the girls." Her husband, for whatever reasons, bought her piece after piece of diamond jewelry, a practice she did not discourage. Even on the tennis court, when she tossed a ball up in the air and served, she sparkled.

The first night she had Annie in her house, Aunt Bunny told her they'd be having Spanish food for dinner.

"Andalusian consommé," she said, "followed by braised rabbit. And for dessert a warm chocolate hazelnut cake with figs and apricots. A little feast we're having in your honor."

When they sat down to eat, the three of them and Annie's cousin, Fleur, Uncle Orel said, "Harumph," and started lecturing, first on the wine he'd chosen to accompany the meal and then on wine in general. Annie heard that wine has "body," "balance," and "complexity," and that it could be "flabby," "silky," "crisp," or "grassy," and that after you drank it, it had "finish." *Duh,* she thought.

When he had finished speaking, Uncle Orel looked at Annie with an expression on his face that she'd seen countless times at school, on the faces of her teachers. It was the "any questions?" look. They *always* wanted questions.

Desperately, she rummaged through her mind in search of something she could ask him.

"Is it true you send your socks to be dry-cleaned?" was the best she could come up with. Her mom had told her that he did, but she had not believed it. Feet got stinky; so did socks. Both needed to be washed.

Uncle Orel blinked and then looked over at his wife. Annie was quite sure he didn't know the answer to her question. Cousin Fleur made a muffled sound. It could have been a laugh, but one she then thought better of.

Cousin Fleur didn't much resemble either of her parents. That was partly by design. Hearing that her sister was trying to get pregnant, Aunt Bunny had decided she would too. She discussed her bright idea with her husband, and the two of them agreed that she should have a daughter, the most beautiful and talented daughter that money could buy.

So, first of all—as Annie's mom explained it—they used "reproductive technology" to improve the odds of Uncle Orel contributing a big majority of X chromosomes to the process of conception. Even more expensive, though, was the "help" they got from a young woman whom Aunt Bunny liked to describe as "a sort of surrogate me." She was a Rhodes Scholarship–winning fashion model who had high cheekbones, a small chin, full lips, long legs, and a tiny waist (none of which described Aunt Bunny), and her SATs had been good enough to put her folder in the "Accept" pile at any college in the Ivy League, as well as Stanford, where she was also captain of the soccer team.

"What they did was implant her—her eggs, that is—inside your aunt and then fertilize them with your uncle's doctored sperm," Annie's mom had told her. "And if that's not cheating, I don't know what is."

But whatever it was, Fleur was born about the same time Annie was, and as the years went by it did seem that the Sachses got their money's worth. Comparisons are odious, Annie knew, but she still couldn't shake the feeling that her mom saw her as Budget Rent a Car, and Fleur as Hertz.

Although Annie had been trained to more or less resent her cousin's looks, she figured it wasn't Fleur's fault that she'd turned out to be a tall, good-looking honor student with a great body who was also very rich. In fact, Annie *liked* Fleur as a person and had come to feel that Fleur liked her.

As if to prove she did, Fleur now turned and winked at Annie. It was a friendly and approving wink. It seemed that Fleur, at least, had thought that Annie'd asked a dandy question.

Not so, Aunt Bunny thought.

"What a person does with socks is really his or her own business," she said rather sternly to her niece. "And not a thing one talks about at dinner. But since you brought the subject up, I'll tell you that your uncle's socks are pure cashmere. *I* send them out to be dry-cleaned and pressed, and then depilled. For your information, that's the way an educated person cares for cashmere socks. What else *would* one do with them?"

That was the last time Annie had a question put to her. In fact, her aunt and uncle talked only to each other during the rest of dinner. Annie got to thinking they really had had Fleur for decoration mostly—someone who could play the part of "daughter" and be admired by their friends. The man who served them dinner, Rollin, was gray and dignified and had an English accent. He was perfect for the part of the "butler"; Annie wondered if he ever "did it." The next morning she had breakfast in the kitchen, in the company of Jean-Batiste, the Sachses' four-star chef, a Frenchman. He told her that preparing food for her was not a part of his *responsabilité*. "I cook only for the mature palate," he said to Annie. "I make that very clear to Madame Sachs. Jean-Batiste does *not* do macaroni-cheese." Beside him on the kitchen counter was a box that, Annie realized, had recently contained *his* breakfast. On the side of it was printed DUNKIN' DONUTS.

By the evening of that day Annie felt herself becoming desperate.

"Everything is just so *perfect* here, even more so than at home," she moaned to Primo. "I can't stand it."

Pantagruel Primo stared at her unblinkingly. "Interesting complaint," he said.

He was propped up on a mahogany side chair in her room that, according to Aunt Bunny, had been personally constructed by Duncan Phyfe, the number one early-American chair guy. Annie was chin-down on the bed but facing toward its foot and him, looking out through the tops of her eyes. Her feet were on either side of her pillow.

"I know, I know," she said dramatically. "How dare I? Here I am, lying on an Orthocomforpedic mattress and a down pillow,"—she kicked it with one clean bare foot—"I'm to be served a gourmet dinner every night, the TV's got DVD, and thanks to the Neversleep Home Protection System, I'm safe from rapists, wolves, and alien or terrorist attack. How can I complain?"

Primo raised his eyebrows but said nothing.

"And, oh yeah," she added, feeling frightfully embarrassed, "no one's cast an awful spell on me."

Her companion nodded, his expression softening.

"So, what is it that you want?" he asked.

"I want to stop feeling how I feel," said Annie. "So much *less*." She gave her delightfully fluffy pillow another kick.

"Less than whom, the Sachses?" Primo wanted to know. "I haven't had much opportunity to study them, but based on first impressions, gleaned when we came in . . ." He made a sour face.

Annie shook her head. "Not less than *them*, exactly. Less than who I *should* be, according to them, who they'd like for me to be. Who my parents keep *expecting* me to become," she said, "the sooner the better. The kid who all the other parents wish they had."

"Do you *want* to be this paragon?" asked Primo. "This perfect being? In their eyes, that is."

"Well, sure," she said. "I *guess*." Her head went down, and when she spoke again, her voice was muffled. "*I* don't know." she looked back up. "Maybe I *don't* want to. Or maybe I don't think I can. I'm really not that good at lots of stuff. I'm pretty doofusy."

"Doofusy?" said Primo. "I don't believe I know—"

"Oh, it just means klutzy," Annie said. She tried again, reaching for a grown-up word. "Incompetent."

"You think you're that?" said Primo. "More so than other people?" Annie nodded. "More so than members of the Dallas Cowboys or the NRA? More so than Hillary or Oprah? More so than Slurpagar the Quaint?"

"For sure," said Annie.

"Well, allow me to be the first to disabuse you of that notion, my dear child," said Primo. "You're not. Of course you *feel* uncomfortable—incompetent—a lot. You're a teenager, for God's sake—how do you think you're meant to feel? But the fact of the matter is, you, me, and every other creature on this planet—including skunks and snails and yellow-shafted flickers—have one thing in common: We will all be good at only three out of every ten things that we try to do. That's part of the 'Unwritten Law'; it's a 'Forget-About-It.'"

"A Forget-About-It?"

"Yes," said Primo. "There are certain things in life that you're incapable of changing, so when you collide with one, the only course of action that makes sense is to just forget about it. Like everybody else, you have things you can be good at and enjoy, and more things that you can't. Your challenge, if you want a seat on the Happiness Express, is to find out what your good things are and then do one or more of them quite often, full-time if possible. But, anyway, we've gotten off the track. You said you wanted to stop feeling *less*. Less than what your parents and the Sachses want or expect you to be. And I asked you if you wanted what they wanted. And you said you didn't know."

"That's right," said Annie. "Part of me would like to. Then they'd be off my back. But it's possible I couldn't do it even if I tried my hardest."

"But how about the part of you that wouldn't like to?" Primo asked. "What's that all about?"

"Oh, I don't know," said Annie. "I feel sort of silly even trying to explain it. It's just a feeling that I have. Of how I'd like to be—'turn out' is how they put it. No one's meant to want to be different, but I think I do, deep down. I want to be the way *I* want to be, I guess."

"Good grief," said Primo, pretending to be shocked. "Am I dealing with a nascent individualist? A person with integrity? A woman with concerns other than the three 'Big Esses': sex and style and schoolwork?"

Annie had to smile. Talking with Primo was definitely making her feel better. When most adults said "Be yourself," they seemed (she thought) to have a particular kind of self in mind, one that they approved of, one that "fit in." Primo—perhaps because he himself, was, a good deal "different"—seemed to think that other people should be different too. He seemed to feel that she should try things out, experiment, and so discover what she truly liked to do and who she really wanted to be.

It was true, she realized, that many of her classmates gave a lot of time and thought to one or more of those three Big Esses. She herself wasn't very big on style. But sex did cross her mind a fair amount, being (as she was) somewhere between virginally curious and cautiously game. And schoolwork . . . well, in part to keep her parents off her back, she most certainly did do her best to always—

"Yikes!" she said out loud. "I just remembered something. I've got English homework for tomorrow. We're meant to write a piece on . . . oh, my god, I can't remember what! She assigned a topic, Mrs. Krump did. She'll kill me if I come in empty-handed!"

"You should *see* the woman," she told Primo. "She has big, long, yellow teeth and a wart on the end of her nose. She's the meanest person in the whole school!"

In fact, the English teacher, Mrs. Krump, was Annie's favorite: a comely blonde with petal skin and an engaging smile, whose husband called her "Peaches." Annie knew what she just said would never be misunderstood by Mrs. Krump. She'd laugh and label it "poetic license."

"I've got to call the Roach Boy," she continued, sliding off the bed. "That's Arby's other name. You remember Arby, right?

My friend from school? I'll explain the Roach Boy business later. I just hope he's home."

"Whoa," said Arby when she had him on the line. "You haven't *started* yet? The topic is 'Life's Darkest Moment.' She said she wanted us to use our best imaginations. And she guaranteed an F to anyone whose story ended with their mother shaking them and they woke up."

"Oof," said Annie. "That's so hard. How's yours going, Arb? You through already?"

"Almost," he said, and proceeded to tell her all about his piece, which was a shortened version of the climax in the novel *Moby Dick*, but told from the point of view of the whale.

Annie said that sounded great, as she'd been pretty sure his story would be. Arby got A's on almost all his stories. He had a great imagination and so was one fantastic writer. Everybody said.

When she hung up, her face, which usually appeared quite round, looked long. And her eyes, which often crinkled at the corners in a smile, were wide with fear. Writing stories wasn't something *she* was great at, ordinarily, and now she had to be imaginative and *fast*. Reverting to type, she worried that she might disgrace herself, her parents (out in Arizona or wherever), and the Sachses. What she'd said to Primo and he'd said to her was—for the moment, anyway—forgotten.

"Well," she told her little friend, "I'm in for it. I have to write a paper on 'Life's Darkest Moment,' which is what this just about is. Except I'm sure Mrs. Krump would hate it if I wrote a piece about a kid writing a piece—and probably half the class has already done that—which is very *un*imaginative. So I haven't a clue what to do. Maybe I should just give up."

"That would be a big mistake," P. P. said. "Giving up almost always is. What I suggest you do is go sit in front of your computer. And then empty your mind. Think of absolutely nothing, if you can. And then, when I say 'Go,' begin to write. Don't worry if it's good or bad, just let the words come out. Allow the Muse to perch upon your shoulder and whisper in your ear."

Having no better idea, Annie did as she was told. Soon, she was writing away, just for the fun of it, it seemed like. Her piece was titled "Life's Darkest Moment?"

6

"Life's Darkest Moment?"
by Annie Ireland

One gloomy February morning [Annie wrote, the words flowing effortlessly from her fingertips and onto the computer's keyboard], a girl named Ashley Ishmael was trudging through the gloomy stretch of forest that lay between the raised ranch in which she lived with her demanding parents and her intimidating high school, Bally High.

"Oh, woe is me," she muttered to herself. "When will I *ever* know which outfit I should wear, figure out how I can do a lot of stuff boys want to do but still stop short of being 'slutty,' do all the work and make the kind of grades my folks demand but at the same time have 'cool' friends *and* reach the point of being popular and 'with it' without inhaling or imbibing or ingesting things I know are not good for my body and my brain cells? In short, how *can* I get the whole world on my side and off my back?"

Ahead of her, just off the path that she was walking on,

she spied the most enormous mushroom that she'd ever seen. It was a good foot and a half high, and its rounded top, bigger even than a barstool's, was smooth and white and—yes!—inviting. Being in no tearing hurry to arrive at school [and be exposed to many different sets of critical opinions], Ashley wandered off the straight and narrow, went up to the giant fungus, and acting on a whim, sat down on it.

She wasn't sure exactly how this happened, but the next thing she knew, she was butt-down on the forest floor, looking at a small man with pointed ears who wore an old top hat and buckles on his shoes and who was standing next to where she sat. There wasn't any mushroom anywhere in sight.

"Who are you?" she asked the little man. "And where's the mushroom I was sitting on?"

"My name is Slurpagar the Quaint," he said. "I am a forest troll. But just last week an enormously gifted . . . colleague [let us say] was mean enough to cast a spell on me. I suppose it was his idea of a joke, or maybe he was simply showing off. In any case, he turned me into a giant mushroom. And the only way I could be changed back into the being that you see before you [according to his stupid spell] would be by having someone—and it had to be a pretty girl—come by and choose to sit on me."

"Wow," said Ashley, blushing a little at the implied compliment. "You might have stayed a mushroom for a good long time. Not many people pass this way, and very few of them are girls."

"I realize that," said Slurpagar the Quaint. "And so I'm

very, very grateful to you. You made—heh-heh—an *excellent* impression on me. And as a token of my gratitude, I'd like to give you something . . . *this*."

He'd reached into an inside pocket as he spoke and now held out an object to her, an object the likes of which she'd seen before.

"It's a . . . *remote*?" said Ashley dubiously. It *looked* like a remote control, in terms of shape and size, but it had only a single button on its face.

"Yes, but it's a *magical* remote," he said. "It's for you to use on *people*, rather than on TVs. If you don't like what someone's saying to you, you just point this little sweetheart at his [or her] head and click. And—just like that!—you've changed their channel. You don't have to listen to their line of crap one second longer."

"You're kidding?" Ashley said excitedly. "That's *huge*. You're *giving* that to me?"

"Yep," said little Slurpagar, "I am. For free. You're looking at *at least* a fifteen-hundred-dollar value, assuming you could find it in a store or on the Shopping Channel, which you couldn't. Plus probably another five ninety-five for shipping and handling if it was in a catalog, which it isn't now and never will be. But now it's yours for nothing, absolutely free. You don't even have to dial a toll-free number!"

"Gee, thanks a whole big bunch," said Ashley. "This ought to come in really, really handy."

"I wouldn't be surprised," the troll agreed. "Though perhaps

you'll be. Now scat! Be on your way before I change my mind and keep this handsome item for myself."

So Ashley slipped the remote in her backpack and took off, continuing her walk to school.

There, she had an ordinary day at first. As usual, she was the object of the sorts of minor put-downs, threats, and insults that were common in the halls of Bally High, but all of them slid off her callused hide today. When she got to Mr. Flesch's English class, however, there was something special waiting for her and the other members of that class: an unannounced and unanticipated test. The question was already written on the board, in Mr. Flesch's rather childlike but achingly legible scrawl:

> In a well-written essay of between one hundred fifty and two hundred words, show how George Eliot's treatment of Silas is concomitant with the cause-and-effect relationship of the protagonist to his heredity and environment.

Ashley stared at the question with a puzzled expression on her face. Even if she knew all the words in it and understood what it was asking for, even if it was possible to show much of anything in an "essay" that short, she *still* couldn't remember anyone named George Eliot or Silas in *A Tale of Two Cities*, which was the novel that the class was reading. And so she raised her hand and said, "I don't understand the question, Mr. Flesch."

Mr. Flesch colored slightly and looked down at her. He

was sitting in a chair behind his desk, which was on a little platform near the chalkboard.

"I'm not surprised," he started. "You see, Miss Ishmael, for one to *inferentiate* the meaning of a *propositary* statement written in the plainest English, one must first . . ."

At which point Ashley, having reached into her backpack and pulled out the troll's remote, aimed it at his head and "changed his channel."

Mr. Flesch stopped talking. Then he got a strange expression on his face, leaned back, and slowly, slowly started sliding down, finally disappearing in the kneehole of his desk.

No sooner had that happened than Tiffany Porringer, the classmate most disposed to pick on Ashley, turned to her and said, "I can't believe you, Ishmael. Bringing your TV remote to *school*? Mr. Flesch is not an entertainment center, *spit-for-brains*."

But then, before she even got to hear the giggle that her clever euphemisms tended to produce, Tiffany pitched forward in her seat. Her forehead thudded on her notebook [fattened by the latest issue of *Cosmo*]. Ashley Ishmael had "changed her channel" too.

When neither Mr. Flesch nor Tiffany got [or sat] right up again, an excited murmur filled the room. A couple of the boys got down on one knee and peered under Flesch's desk at the motionless teacher, and a large girl named Vidalia Thrumming took it upon herself to go up to Tiffany, bend over, latch onto her wrist, and whisper something in her ear. Only three or four of the most committed suck-butts, with desperate expressions on their faces, actually tried to start writing the essay.

When Tiffany stayed motionless, Vidalia straightened up and told the class, "I do believe this child has passed."

And so she had, the teacher, too, neither with a mark on them. But their "channels" had been "changed" [alive to dead].

Though witnesses did testify that Ashley Ishmael had pointed a remote at both of them, no law enforcement person was about to risk public ridicule by saying *that* had caused their deaths. The remote was seized as "evidence" by the police, but it "disappeared" from the chief's desk before he could try it out or send it to the FBI crime lab in Washington, D.C. For this, he blamed the cleaning woman. A coroner's jury concluded that the victims died of "unknown causes."

Ashley was sorry Tiffany and Mr. Flesch had died, but she couldn't really blame herself. The person who had caused their deaths, she felt, was that irresponsible little Slurpagar the Quaint. *She'd* thought he'd given her a magical [but harmless] toy, not a lethal weapon. *He'd* known what was sure to happen when she "changed their channels."

One interesting effect of this whole . . . incident was that the other kids became a good deal less inclined to pick on Ashley Ishmael. Another was that Mrs. Varneigh, who succeeded Mr. Flesch, never got Charles Dickens's work confused with *Silas Marner*.

So, all in all, the passing of her teacher and her classmate was not, for Ashley Ishmael, "Life's Darkest Moment."

7

Getting Reviewed

As soon as Annie finished printing out "Life's Darkest Moment?" she read it out loud to her captive audience, Pantagruel Primo, Esquire.

In the course of the writing she'd gotten prouder and prouder of herself, of what she was doing, so now she wanted to hear the story read out loud, in its entirety. She also wanted to hear what Primo would say when he heard it, what he'd think of it. And finally, she wanted to be sure that he agreed with her about its authorship.

She'd decided *she* believed the piece was hers. She didn't doubt that he'd *inspired* her, nor did she for a moment deny he'd made *her* write it. She was convinced that he had "powers," that he could, for instance, cast a spell on her that'd make her a better writer. But it wasn't Pantagruel Primo who'd sat down at the computer and typed out "Life's Darkest Moment?" *She'd* done that. She hadn't copied or stolen it from any other writer; it was her baby (even more than he was, absolutely). She wasn't any plagiarist, and *he* wasn't any artificial inseminationist.

She cleared her throat and started reading.

Primo turned out to be an excellent audience. He may have looked like a baby, but in fact, he was a critic cut from the same cloth as . . . oh, Rex Reed, or maybe Siskel and Roeper.

"Four stars!" he enthused when she was done. "An imaginative and quirky cautionary tale! Surefire teen magnetism!" And then, in a more conversational tone of voice, "I'd say you were quite kind to Slurpagar the Quaint, however, by not making even more of an issue of his role in the tragedy. *He'd* probably call it 'mischievous,' his giving the remote to a kid like Ashley without telling her what it could do to someone. But in my book the little squirt was downright unprofessional, bordering on demonic. Guys have been suspended from the brotherhood for less than that."

Annie nodded. Inside, she'd been delighted when she heard him say "*you* were quite kind to Slurpagar the Quaint." Clearly, he, too, saw the piece as hers, not his. And, of course, she *loved* his liking it.

"If you don't mind," she then said to him, "I'd like to call up Arby and read it to him, too. Can you stand to hear it again? I could take the phone into the bathroom." By then Annie had become quite conscious of the fact that, unlike everybody else she knew, he couldn't storm out of a room when he got sick of someone. Talk about a major handicap! That would be even worse than losing one's ability to slam doors.

"No, no," he said quite cheerfully. "By all means, read away. I'm sure I'll like it even more the second time."

Annie smiled. She wasn't used to compliments from grown-ups she was living with. This was really nice. "I just hope he's up still," she said as she dialed the number.

The Roach Boy *was* up—or at least he said he was. That was a thing about their friendship. Each of them tried very hard to "be there" for the other.

She read the piece out loud again.

"Oh, Annie," Arby said when she had finished. "I absolutely *love* it! I'm pretty sure that it's your best one yet!"

His praise made Annie glow. The long face that she'd grown before she started writing had become quite round again; her eyes had regained their sparkle. Though only a freshman, Arby had already had pieces of his published in *Converse-ing*, Converse High School's literary magazine. He was a Someone in the world of Y.A. literature.

"I can't wait for Mrs. Krump to read this one," he said. "She is going to *flip*. And I bet you had a ball writing it too. The thing is, when you get a great idea like this, the piece almost writes itself, don't you think?"

"Um, yeah," said Annie. She almost told him then and there about the "help" she'd (sort of) gotten. But then she decided that'd be a complication, a distraction. She wanted nothing more, right then, than to just kick back and wallow in the warmth of his approval.

• • •

Arby was right. Mrs. Estelle "Peaches" Krump admired "Life's Darkest Moment?" every bit as much as he did. And because she was the faculty adviser to *Converse-ing*, she was able to shoehorn Annie's piece into the very next issue.

Annie counted the days to publication. She couldn't wait. She was going to send a copy to her parents by Express Mail. For once, they'd both be proud of her. She dared to hope that this, like the election of President James Monroe in 1816, would usher in a whole new "era of good feeling."

On the same day Annie sent the little magazine winging toward her irritable-from-hunger parents out at Negative Feedback, another copy of *Converse-ing* was carried home by Converse High eleventh grader Bettina Bloomingdale, who had in it her environmentally sensitive poem titled "Drek." (Black is the odor of our screwed-up air . . . ," it began.)

She left it in the front hall, lying on the bench right next to the hall closet, feeling that her father couldn't help seeing it there when he arrived home from the office. She was sure that her dad would *hate* her poem and that reading it might ruin his appetite, something she was all in favor of. She always ate her kind of food up in her room, while he devoured bloody steaks and chops and roasts downstairs.

D'Artagnan Arminius Bloomingdale, Bettina's father, suspected that his daughter did a lot of things just to annoy him. This was a habit, or possibly a trait (he felt), that she'd picked up from Raquel, his wife, her mother. His counter to the two of them was to never be annoyed—or at least to make sure that his annoyance never showed.

His father had named him after two heroes, one fictional and one real: the swashbuckling D'Artagnan from *The Three Musketeers*, by Alexandre Dumas; and the daring, brilliant tribal chief Arminius (aka Hermann the German), who, in the year A.D. 9, dealt the Roman legions a crushing defeat in the Teutoburg Forest. So Bloomingdale decided early on that he'd be a hero in his own right. His first two initials gave him the idea of just what kind of hero he should be: an incorruptible crime-fighting district attorney who'd lead a crusade that would transform Converse County into the safest and most law-abiding district in the land. No criminal, real or potential, rich or poor, young or old, slick or clumsy, out or closeted, would be beyond his reach or notice.

And that went double for the disrespectful, often homicidal, teenagers whose appearance was a blot on the natural landscape and whose foulmouthed lawlessness all too frequently earned them no more than a slap on the wrist from lily-livered law enforcement figures.

When he found that copy of *Converse-ing* in the exact same spot where he liked to set his briefcase down every night, he smiled a thin-lipped smile (even as his insides raged: *How* dare *she?*). He knew full well who'd put it there, and why.

That night, when his wife turned on the TV (an episode of *Antiques Roadshow*), he strolled out of the room (whistling merrily) and repaired to his study, where he opened *Converse-ing* and read his daughter's poem. He thought that "Drek" was appropriately titled but otherwise completely lacking in merit; indeed, he was disgusted by its pro-clean air and antibusiness message. But that didn't keep him from writing Bettina a short note ("Read your *delightful* poem. Move over, Emily Dickinson! Bravo!" signed "Your proud Pa"), which he later left on the hall carpet, right outside her bedroom door.

Then, having little else to do, he started reading other selections in *Converse-ing*. He felt that most of them were the kind of teenage tripe one would expect to find in a high school literary magazine. But then he read "Life's Darkest Moment?"

"Well, well, well," he said out loud when he had finished it. "What have we here?"

His chief investigator would have recognized that tone of voice. District Attorney Bloomingdale had someone in his sights, someone who, in his opinion, posed a threat to law and order in the county.

8.

The D.A. Takes Aim

Louie Scanlon was the district attorney's chief investigator. He was a totally inconspicuous and exceptionally boring man who happened to be very good at "looking into things," like other people's business. D.A. Bloomingdale had told him that he needed "the full skinny" on "the suspect, this Ann Ireland." It didn't take Lou Scanlon long to come up with a thin manila folder's worth of yawn-provoking information. The girl was only in her middle teens; she was much too young to have an interesting past.

"To begin with," Scanlon droned, "the subject of this inquiry turns out to be a female and Caucasian. That she is of the gentle sex would be atypical, given the nature of the crime we're looking into. But her color is statistically appropriate, I'd say."

"Yes, yes, yes. Go on," the D.A. said impatiently, tapping the edge of a yellow legal pad with a number two Ticonderoga yellow wooden pencil. *A female and Caucasian? Judas Priest,* he thought. Scanlon's thoroughness could be annoying at times.

Of course an "Ann" would be a female, and someone by the name of Ireland (like that Kathy in his old *Sports Illustrated* swimsuit issues) would almost certainly be white all over.

Scanlon then shuffled through the papers in his folder and proceeded to read off a long list of further facts about "the suspect," things like her height and weight and date of birth, the color of her hair and eyes, her hobbies and her allergies, her favorite fast food, sport, TV show, recording artist, month of the year, soft drink, brand of underpants, and Ben & Jerry's flavor (Phish Food).

At the end of all that he said, "As far as residence is concerned, you 'member that nice house burned down last month? Just past Poplar on South Prospect? The big old center-hall colonial, with five bedrooms, four baths, master suite, library, central air, and a recently remodeled kitchen? On a full two-acre lot, nicely landscaped, with heated pool, two-car garage, and views of—"

"Right. Yeah, sure. I *do* remember," the D.A. interrupted. At the time of the fire he'd felt a momentary pang of sympathy for the owners of the place. Given its location, they probably were voters who'd supported him.

"Well, people name of Ireland owned it," Scanlon told him. "And it turns out this here Caucasian female suspect, Ann, would be their daughter."

"Ah, is that *so*?" Bloomingdale beamed, suddenly alert and interested. "If she's a native of *that* neighborhood, she might be perfect in more ways than one."

For quite some time the editors of the *Converse Tribune*, a left-leaning rag in the D.A.'s opinion, had made a point of his "habitual targeting" (their words) of the county's poorest citizens in his prosecutions. So he'd been hoping that there'd fall into his lap an open-and-shut case, hopefully involving drugs, in which the "perp" would be (let's say) a college kid—one whose photo in the *Tribune* would show him in a tweed jacket, Dockers, tasseled loafers, and no socks, in addition to the cuffs and shackles. That'd not only take care of the "habitual targeting" business, but it would also show that the D.A. was a frontline compassionate commando in the war on drugs. The way he figured it, everyone (except maybe the kid and his parents) would agree he needed to be put away awhile, for his sake and society's.

Although Ann Ireland wasn't male, a college student, or involved with drugs, she still (he thought) could serve his purposes. She would be perceived as "upper class," a shopper at the Gap, and she was guilty of another thing the public Wanted Something Done About. Shootings in schools around the country were a hot topic and had gotten so much unfavorable attention that even this perp's gender wouldn't earn her any sympathy. Ever since the state of Texas executed that nicelooking, born-again killer gal, John and Jane Doe had come to terms with the fact that the female of the species was as dangerous as the male—and should be held equally responsible. That was, at least, what D.A. Bloomingdale believed.

"Although the parents of the suspect are no longer in the county or the state," the chief investigator continued, "having left a short while after the incendiary incident for a sojourn at a health spa in the great Southwest, *she* is still domiciled in this jurisdiction, at the home of her maternal aunt and uncle, a Mr. and Mrs. Orel Sachs."

"Indeed?" his boss said thoughtfully. He knew the Sachses, not as *friends*, exactly, but what he called "semisocially," as a result of "common interests." In other words, they were major contributors to the political party under whose banner he was proud to run. "I think I'd better give Br'er Sachs a call."

And he made a flicking, shooing motion with one hand that told Lou Scanlon it was time for him to leave the office. He left so inconspicuously, the D.A. didn't even notice he was gone.

It wasn't hard to get in touch with Orel Sachs. His business was "investments," and he took care of business either in his home, attired in a velvet smoking jacket, or sometimes on the golf course, where he wore plus fours and often used a five wood off the fairway. This day, he was at home, working on his billiards game, but the D.A.'s phone call was a welcome interruption. In fact, he'd gotten tired of standing up and leaning over.

After some opening chitchat about the unpredictable nature of the local weather, Bloomingdale steered the conversation onto a different subject, but one that also wasn't always easy to make book on: the behavior of the politicians in their statehouse.

"I thought you'd like to know," he told Ann Ireland's uncle, "that our people in the house have finally put together a bill that'll allow me to get tough on young offenders. I believe it comes up for a vote today. After that it ought to breeze right through the senate, and the governor has said he'll sign it."

"Good *job*," said Annie's uncle heartily. "Ugly little bastards seem to be everywhere these days. I can't even stand to look at them, with their baggy pants and all their pierced whatevers! Did you know a hundred people surveyed rated 'teenage kids' *second* (after 'dog poop' but ahead of 'potholes') as the most unpleasant hazard on the city's streets?"

"Um, no," the D.A. said, "I didn't. Interesting. But speaking of that breed of cat—of young offenders in the county—there's something that I wanted to run by you and get your thinking on." He'd gotten to the edge of thin ice, the D.A. knew. He crossed the fingers of the hand that didn't hold the phone and then, just for the fun of it, his eyes.

"Of course," said the generous Mr. Sachs. "Go right ahead."

"Well, sir, it is this," said the nervous Bloomingdale. "No point trying to gild the bush or beat around the lily. Heh-heh-heh. But it's come to my attention that someone in your household, a young woman, a juvenile, has committed—made—a . . . bad misstep. She's in some pretty 'deep doo-doo,' as the kids say nowadays, and I'm not referring here to canine . . . droppings."

Because Orel Sachs didn't think of Annie Ireland as a member of his "household"—indeed, he frequently forgot that she existed—and because he was pretty darn sure that the cunning upstairs maid, Felicia, was no juvenile (despite her saucy ways), he just assumed the district attorney was referring to his daughter, Fleur.

"Surely not," he said. "That's unbelievable. There must be some mistake. Let me get Bunny on the other line. I'm sure that if the three of us can take a moment here, just put our heads together . . ."

Bloomingdale heard a click, then nothing for a while, followed by two more clicks and the angry voice of Bunny Sachs.

"Is that you, Artie?" she said, using the D.A.'s detested nickname. "What's this nonsense Orel's telling me about?"

"I'm afraid it isn't nonsense," he said, staying calm and dignified. "She wrote a little allegory that's a thinly veiled warning to the teachers and the students at her school, a warning that she's comtemplating shooting them. And it's been published in the school's literary magazine. In light of what's been going on around the country, we have to take that seriously."

"Don't be an ass," said Bunny Sachs. "She'd never put anything like that in writing, even if she thought it was a good idea. She's much too sensible and cautious. Some feebleminded little fool is trying to play a joke on her—some computer hacker or whatever they're called, probably. You don't have this in her *hand*writing, I bet. You've got nothing you could prove in court, admit it, Artie. Our lawyers'd chew you up and spit you out in little pieces. It'd be the end of your career; you'd be a laughingstock. Fleur isn't any sacrificial lamb, some little skateboard punk from the north end. She just happens to be about the most admired and respected student—by kids *and* teachers—in her whole damn school!"

District Attorney Bloomingdale switched the phone to his other hand and dried the first one on the side of his trousers. What a lioness the woman was! He pitied the poor hunter (not him, for sure!) who might try to harm *her* cub. But what Bunny's last sentences had made him realize was that he'd been terribly misunderstood.

"Wait," he told her now. "Hold on." He even managed a chuckle. "I'm not talking about your *Fleur*. Of course I know what kind of kid *she* is. This is about your niece, Ann Ireland. I've been told she's living in your house now. Isn't that correct?"

He thought he heard two whooshing exhalations of relief as he was saying that. He'd stupidly forgotten that the Sachses even had a daughter. Now what he had to do was cross his fingers one more time and hope that they were much, much less protective of their niece.

"Oh, yes—*Annie*," said her uncle. He said her name sort of in the way that people say "strep throat" or "hemorrhoids." "What *is* it that she's done, again?"

"We don't really know her very well," put in Aunt Bunny. "We agreed to take her in after the fire, when her parents had to go away. We don't know much about her, really. I think Fleur tries to help her get along in school, but that's the way our Fleursie *is*. She's nice to *everyone*! So, what *is* it Annie did?"

The district attorney repeated what he'd said before, describing

Annie's "crime" in a little more detail, how she'd written this "story" in which a girl—a girl much like herself—did away with a teacher and a classmate, sort of "accidentally on purpose." He said he planned to prosecute the case in adult court.

"Kids haven't been getting the message," he said wearily. "It's almost as if they think they *can* get away with murder—or at least planning it. But if I read him right, I'd say Judge Rowland is about ready to make an example of someone, if he has to. Show young people that even in a civilized, compassionate society, there are dire consequences when you cross the line."

There was a silence after that. A *respectful* silence, Bloomingdale believed. It was as if the Sachses, both of them, were now a little bit in awe of him. He liked that.

"You don't suppose . . ." It was Annie's uncle Orel, speaking slowly, with a little quaver in his voice. "I mean, I know the legislature reinstated it, because they knew the people *wanted* it, but in a case like this you wouldn't, would you . . . ?"

"Seek the death penalty?" the D.A. finished for him. "Oh, Lordy no." It occurred to him it was a good thing that being an idiot didn't interfere with someone's ability to write checks. "Nothing like that. A few days in county jail is all we'll go for, I imagine. But she'll be doing real time, in the company of real criminals. It won't be anything like 'Camp Slapawrista,' as I like to call our juvenile detention center. When she gets out and tells her friends what it's like in there, they should think twice before they dare mess up."

"I bet you're right," said Bunny Sachs. "Kids need to have

a good scare thrown at them. I'm shocked that Annie'd write something like what you said. Not that I believe she'd ever really *kill* someone. But it's beyond me where kids these days get some of their ideas. Why, when *we* were young, about the worst thing anybody did was write 'Mr. Rumpert is a big fat fairy' on his blackboard. And face it, everybody *knew* he was a flamer."

"Hmm, yes," the D.A. said. "Well, times have changed, I guess. I'll probably be seeing you in court. Hate to put you through this kind of thing, but if I know Judge Rowland, he won't keep you long."

That really went quite well, he thought as he hung up.

9.

Trial and . . .

It was on a Wednesday, at almost the end of the school day, that Annie Ireland's social studies teacher, after answering a knock on the classroom door, told her to report to the principal's office. She couldn't imagine why. Some helpful classmates, though, went "Ooh" and "Aah" and ran stiff fingers straight across their throats.

Waiting for her in the office were State Troopers Henry C. Bobb and Marcus G. Ray, who told her she was under arrest and should come along with them to the county courthouse.

At first, she thought this was some kind of a joke, orchestrated by the Roach Boy, probably. He was the only person she could think of who was imaginative and ingenious enough to conceive of, and then pull off, a prank of this magnitude.

So she walked to the state police cruiser smiling, flanked by Bobb and Ray and carrying Pantagruel Primo, who was giving her some looks she took to mean *I am not liking this*.

When they arrived at the courthouse, she found her aunt

and uncle standing grimly in the hall, and the sight of them informed her that Primo had been right: This was not a joke. Aunt Bunny and Uncle Orel were beyond solemn. They had on this-isn't-any-laughing-matter looks, blended with how-could-you? glares.

"I tried to reach your mother," Aunt Bunny said, giving her niece a glancing hug and an air kiss. "But they're both sub-merged in mud baths for the day."

"We've made arrangements," Uncle Orel added, "to have you represented legally. I'm sure whomever the judge appoints will know the best way to proceed, in a matter of this sort."

On their way to the courthouse the Sachses had decided they certainly weren't going to ask anyone from *their* law firm, Hyde Royce Pommery Hatch, to dirty his hands on Annie's problem. Hyde Royce did not concern itself with adolescent recklessness or spitting on the subway.

"Really, Annie," her mother's sister added, "what were you *thinking* of? Do you realize how embarrassing this will be for *Fleur*?"

"I don't understand what's going on," said Annie. "The troopers said this has to do with something I wrote for English class. What did I do—split an infinitive? Since when is bad grammar a crime?" She really didn't get it, at that point in time.

"You're charged with being a threat to public safety," Uncle Orel said. "And it looks as if you may be. I understand that you wrote that it is all right for a high school student—a girl like you—to kill her teachers and her classmates. Personally, I can't *imagine* where you got such an idea. Not from anyone in *our* house, surely."

"What?" said Annie. "Me—a threat to public safety? That's ridiculous. I never said it was okay to kill anyone—I never would!"

She was outraged, close to tears. Then suddenly it dawned on her that they must be thinking about her little story, "Life's Darkest Moment?" But it had been in the school's literary magazine, for heaven's sake. That meant it was *good*, not something you could get arrested for. How could literature be thought of as a threat to public safety?

At that point someone sidled up to her. He looked to be a person in his thirties, but one who hadn't ever surfed on any wave of national prosperity. He had on a dark suit that could have used a trip to the dry cleaner's—as could his greasy-looking long straight hair, for that matter. He had a slip of paper in his hand.

"Miss *Iceland*?" he said to Annie. "Miss Ann Iceland?" She thought that if she answered *Boo!* he'd take off running. He had a worse complexion than any boy in her class, except for Reed Blemisch.

But instead, she told him, "No, but I'm Ann *Ireland*."

He blinked at her. Then he lifted up the slip of paper and peered at it more closely.

"Oh," he said, "that's right. Ann *Ireland*." He laughed nervously. "Can't even read my own writing."

Annie didn't say anything. She couldn't imagine what this obvious loser wanted. Pantagruel Primo, in her arms, looked as if he might throw up.

"I'm Luther Pendragin," the young man told her. "I've been assigned to represent you."

"You're a *lawyer?*" Annie asked him. She knew she'd sounded astonished, and she hadn't meant to be rude, but this person wasn't at all what she thought lawyers looked like. In fact, put him in the proper uniform, and he'd be about right for someone who hoped to work his way up to assistant manager at a McDonald's.

"Yes," Pendragin said, "I am . . . an attorney in private practice here in Converse County and a member of the local bar. I've been assigned to your case, and I'm afraid you've gotten yourself into some pretty hot water here. This isn't what I'd call a great time to be advocating school violence." He shook his head back and forth, looking mournful. "Not that any time really is, when you think about it. So how were you thinking of pleading?"

"What?" said Annie. "Pleading? I never advocated school violence. That's completely crazy; I just told my aunt and uncle that. How do you *think* I'm pleading? I'm totally innocent. All I've done is write a story. A *good* story. It was in the school's literary magazine."

Pendragin made a face, a "so what?" sort of face. "Uh-huh," he said. He'd taken out a little notebook and a ballpoint pen. "Okay. Now tell me this. Have you—or anyone in your family—

ever been treated for a mental illness? They ever send you to the school psychologist? Even that might help our cause a little."

Of course Annie guessed what he was getting at. She'd heard of the "insanity defense." This joke of a lawyer was acting as if he thought she *was* guilty of something.

"Look," she said, "Mr. Pendragin, I'm not crazy. I've never seen the school psychologist. I'm absolutely not guilty. Anyone with any common sense would know that if they read my story. This is all on account of that story I wrote, isn't it? Have you read the story yourself? Use a little common sense, can't you?"

"Well, um . . . Miss Ireland," he said. "What you have to understand is that this isn't about common sense. The prosecution is going to claim that in addition to advocating school violence, your story subtly endorses drug use by its mention of a magical mushroom and also glorifies the triumph of evil over good by showing how easily and effectively a little demon can manipulate a human being and not be punished for so doing."

"And I happen to know," put in Uncle Orel, who'd been eavesdropping on their conversation, "that the legislature's just now passing some new laws that'll make a lot of things that you kids do a crime. People are up to here"—he held an open palm sideways, just below his chin—"with having to put up with teenage terrorism. I'm afraid your timing couldn't have been worse on this one!"

That was the last straw, having her uncle say something like that. Annie burst into tears. Obviously, Uncle Orel had already passed judgment on her. He'd decided she was guilty of a crime. She clutched P. Primo to her bosom and sobbed onto his hard little head. All her life, she'd done her best to please her parents and other grown-ups. She'd thought that getting a story in her school's literary magazine would be just the sort of thing they'd *love* to have her do. But instead of . . . well, respect and admiration, it looked as if what she was going to get was, like, abandonment and condemnation. This seemed to her to be the darkest moment in a life that hadn't known a lot of bright ones.

She didn't remember the next half hour all that clearly, but she did retain the gist of what happened. She was brought before an official-looking person who went "blah-blah-blah . . . a threat to public safety" and who asked her how she wished to plead. She moaned out something that her "lawyer," this Luther Pendragin, translated as "She wants to plead not guilty" (while shaking his head), and the official-looking person answered "blah-blah-blah for trial on such and such a date," and he then concluded with some more blah-blahing that remanded her to the custody of her aunt and uncle, Mr. and Mrs. Sachs.

At the end of all that they, minus the lawyer, got into the Sachses' car, and Aunt Bunny drove them home, with Annie and Primo curled up into a miserable ball in the backseat.

10.

. . . Punishment

It wasn't until they got up to Annie's room that Pantagruel Primo was able to express himself (out loud) concerning all he'd witnessed in the course of that long afternoon.

"Splutrisplitz!" he went, spraying Annie (much to her surprise) with a heartfelt and volcanic Bronx cheer. "Never in my life," he exclaimed, "have I observed stupidity of such an Everestian height! Do you realize what I'm saying? I've been watching human ignorami for generations. I watched them vote in Prohibition in this country; I thought I'd seen it all. But what I saw today was like a new gold dollar in the Bank of the Absurd. How anyone could read that lovely little story of yours and think that it was advocating *anything* . . . is totally beyond me. Look, I'll grant you: Slurpagar the Quaint is no tall redwood in the Yocomprendo Forest, but even he knows irony and humor when it pulls his pants down from behind."

Little Primo's outrage was so sincere, and his condemnation so encompassing, that Annie managed a wan smile.

"I'm just so glad you're here," she told her erstwhile baby. "If I were all alone, I don't know what I might be thinking. Probably that I'd gone crazy, just like my lawyer wishes that I had."

"Ha!" barked Primo. "The insanity defense! What a booby-hatchian suggestion *that* was! That silly little ambulance chaser should consider it for himself—to defend him from the wrath of Primo!" He made a few more loud Bronx cheers; they seemed to calm him down a little.

"Look, what I suggest is this: Call up Arby," he went on. "Get him over here. He's a good, bright lad. Perhaps if we three put our heads together, talk this whole thing over . . ."

He didn't sound too hopeful, Annie thought.

Arby came right over. He had things in common with the roaches he hung out with sometimes. Notable among them (in addition to a liking for spaghetti) was; he *could* move very quickly. Now he listened, his face a mask of horror, as Annie told her story.

"This isn't possible," he said when she was done. "Things like this can't happen in the U.S.A. This is the land of liberty and justice for all."

"Um, well, perhaps we shouldn't base our whole defense on *that*," said Primo. "I love your Constitution and its Bill of Rights, and if I had to be a citizen of anywhere, I absolutely would choose here. But it seems to me you don't do as well as you might when it comes to crime and punishment."

"How d'you mean?" said Arby, a tad defensively.

"Well," said Primo, "if he feels like it, that judge can toss dear Annie in the calaboose. And she *is* innocent, purer than the driven snow. If anyone is guilty of what they charged her with, it's Thalia, the Muse of comedy—or me!" He paused and thought about that. "Or maybe Slurpagar the Quaint, who's responsible for my being here in the first place."

"Or how about *me*?" said Arby. "I could have given her a different story idea—maybe something about her pet snail dying, something totally harmless like that. She called me up, and all I did was babble on about what *I* was doing. She was in a time fix and she needed help. I wasn't any help at all."

When he stopped talking, he bit his lower lip and dropped his head for a moment. Annie got a lump in her throat from thinking about how he and Pantagruel Primo had to be about the best friends a girl could ever have.

The Roach Boy then looked up again and stared at Primo.

"I probably shouldn't even ask this," he said, "but, well, I gotta. You have special powers, way beyond what other kinds of people have. So can't you do something that'd kinda *fix* this situation? Can't you get Annie out of this mess?"

Pantagruel Primo sighed. "You're right in saying I have special powers. If, for example, Annie had been captured by some cackling archfiend and now lay bound and gagged and stretched across some railroad tracks with a freight train bearing down on her . . . well, I could turn that forty-eight-car freight into a caterpillar. And it'd crawl right over her, as pretty as you please, and never even tickle!"

"So . . . yes?" said Arby hopefully.

"But," Primo continued, "I myself am bound by many rules and regulations. You should see our Mellow Pages, our big book of operating instructions. It's so fat, housewives use it for a step stool. On page one it reminds us all: 'You're good, but you're not God.' One of the things we're expressly forbidden to do is interfere with any country's laws and their enforcement. I could create . . . distractions in the courtroom, but that'd mostly be a waste of time and energy. I can't stop the trial or change the judge's sentence.

"I'll tell you one thing, though," he added, looking up at Annie. "Somehow, I'll stick with you, come what may. You have my word on that. I may be limited by rules and regs, but there's still lots that I can do to help—I hope."

"I can't thank you both enough," said Annie. "I haven't got a clue about what's apt to happen next, but, well . . . I'm going to do my best to *not* be a doofus while it's happening."

"You go, girl," said the Roach Boy, grinning at her.

"Figurative high five," appended the immobile Primo.

Luther Pendragin did nothing to lift Annie's spirits when she saw him for the second time, right before the trial. He wore the same baggy brown suit (with a new little crust of dried-out food—Chinese?—on one lapel) and the same air of uncertainty.

"I tried to work out a plea bargain with the D.A.?" he informed her hesitantly, making a question of that statement of fact.

"And he told me I could file whatever I wanted to propose 'where the sun don't shine.' Well, I *assumed* he meant at one of those subterranean offices in the city hall basement, but when I took my proposal down there, nobody knew what I was talking about." He shook his head and looked bewildered.

"So I suppose you'll still be wanting to plead not guilty?" he went on. "I just hope that doesn't irritate the judge too much. I'm not going to call you as a witness, not only 'cause I'm sure Bloomingdale'd turn you into wet toilet paper with his cross-exam, but also 'cause they tell me anything that drags things out sends Judge Rowland into a towering rage. And that's the last thing that I want to do, believe me."

It seemed to Annie that Judge Rockford N. Rowland ("Ol' Rock-'n'-Roll" to courthouse regulars) was already in a towering rage when he stomped into the courtroom. He read the charges against "the defendant, Ann Ireland" in a disgusted snarl. They were a long hodgepodge of legalese, on the one hand (featuring expressions like "reckless disregard"), and personal prejudice ("potty-mouthed pathology"), on the other. Exhibit A, the only one, was Annie's story.

Judge Rowland finished with a question, aimed at Luther Pendragin. "So what's the plea here, buster?"

"If it please the court," Pendragin whined, pulling at his forelock, "not guilty."

Judge Rowland snorted in surprise, then growled at the attorney, "Prove it."

Pendragin stalled. He opened his attaché case, which was

lying on the table in front of him. Annie and Primo—though not the judge—could see it contained only a homemade baked-bean sandwich on Wonder bread in a plastic Baggie and a Hostess Twinkie. Primo wrinkled up his nose and stared at both food items. In a moment a worm —a black-headed white grub, actually—was seen to push its way out of the sandwich's filling, and the little cake turned into what appeared to be . . . dog doo-doo.

"Well," Pendragin finally muttered, "all she did was write a story. It got into her high school literary magazine." He didn't seem to notice that his lunch had been . . . transformed. He didn't even seem to hear the little song Primo was singing, sotto voce. ". . . play pinochle up your snout," it ended.

"So all she did was write a *story*," said the judge, "that got into a *literary* magazine. Now isn't that *creative* of her?" He snorted. "Well, I can be creative too. Let me tell you how this story's going to end. Ann Ireland, rise and face the court."

She did.

"I sentence you to five days in the county jail," he said. "And you damn well better tell your literary friends that your story-telling days are over!"

Annie's parents weren't in the courtroom. They'd called her up the night before and explained that their final weigh-in at Negative Feedback would also be taking place the following morning. This, they said, would be the high point—indeed, the big excitement—of their stay, the moment when they found out how much their suffering (and consequent weight loss) was going to set them back. They knew she wouldn't want them to miss out on that.

"You won't even recognize your father," said her mother. "I can't wait to see the expression on your face when you see both of us. And don't worry about your hearing, or whatever it is. We're sure that you'll do fine."

11.

Aftermath

Though Annie's parents weren't present in the courtroom during her sentencing, the Roach Boy had a front-row seat. To say he found fault with Judge Rowland's resolution of the case is like saying a Godiva chocolate is a mildly good-tasting sweet.

"You're sentencing her to five days in the county jail?" he shouted, standing up. "That *sucks*! I've read that story! It's fantastic writing! You can't send a kid to jail for being excellent in English. Annie Ireland isn't any criminal, she's a real good kid. Grown-ups get to write—or say—all kinds of hateful stuff, and nothing's done to stop them. But let a kid make a joke that grown-ups take the wrong way, and she gets tossed in jail. That really *sucks*!"

And he sat down, panting.

"Are you done?" asked Judge Rowland pleasantly. He stretched his mouth into a thin-lipped smile. "Are you sure there's nothing else you'd like to say? Some further exercise of what you probably imagine to be your First Amendment rights? Have you no more instructions and critiques you'd like to give this court?"

"No," said Arby in a small voice, staying seated. He was having trouble realizing he'd said what he just said. Talking back to people in authority was not a skill he'd practiced much.

"Then suck on *this*," Judge Rowland said, sounding quite delighted with himself. "I find *you* guilty of contempt of court, you unruly little whippersnapper. And so I also sentence *you* to five days in our county lockup. Let this day be known as the end of coddle time for kids in Converse County!"

A pair of heavyset deputies collected Arby from his front-row seat and led him out the side door of the courtroom. He thought he should shout out something as he left, a penetrating question on the subject of fairness or a defiant statement on the order of "Give me liberty or give me death." But the only famous words he could think of (beside that old chestnut) were "Did somebody say McDonald's?" so he stayed silent. He hoped the smile he plastered on his face would cover up the fact that he was scared to death.

At that point a very properly dressed middle-aged woman in the very back of the courtroom stood up.

"Excuse me, Your Honor," she said. "But may I have your permission to address the court at this time?"

Judge Rowland peered down from the bench, no longer looking pleased.

"Will someone have the goodness to explain to me what's going on?" he asked rhetorically. "Is there some sort of anarchists' convention currently in progress locally? This is a court of law. As the judge, I am in charge. Prosecutors, witnesses, and attorneys are allowed to speak—defendants, if they wish to, too. But comments from the peanut gallery are neither solicited nor welcome, madam. I've been running things around here for a good long while, and I'm quite sure I don't need any help from *you*!"

"I agree. Indeed you don't, Your Honor," said the woman. "Your name, in my opinion, is synonymous with law and order in the county. I think you do a fourteen-carat *sterling* job. The only reason why I asked your permission to speak is that I'm Ms. Persimmon—Gladys Persimmon," she simpered, "Annie Ireland's Life Skills teacher at the high school, a fellow professional, like yourself. Well, what I wanted to say was, an important part of our curriculum, what we call the 'lab portion' of the class," she tittered, "is going on right now, as we speak. The girls are all required, for this entire term, to take care of 'babies'—which are dolls, of course—one of which, as you can see, Miss Ireland is cuddling at this very moment. Studies have shown that girls who complete this section of the course have a lower instance of undesired pregnancies or later instances of child abuse, not to mention drugs and alcohol. So what I was hoping was that you'd see fit to permit Ann Ireland to take her 'baby' with her and to keep on tending it while she serves the time in jail to which you justifiably and judiciously have just sentenced her. I thank you."

Judge Rowland took a deep breath. Then he puffed his

cheeks way out and exhaled suddenly, making a popping sound. His Honor was fed up (as well as flattered).

"Oh, all right, all *right*," he said. "Never let it be said that this court doesn't support educational . . . innovations, no matter how wacko they may seem to be." He turned to the court reporter. "Let the record show that Ann Ireland's ersatz baby is hereby ordered to serve her sentence with her."

He then stood up, picked up his little wooden hammer, and gave the gavel a good rap.

"And that's all the justice for today," he said, and exited the courtroom.

Annie looked down at Pantagruel Primo, Esquire. He had a broad smile on his face and his baby blues were twinkling.

"That lady, Ms. Persimmon," she said. "She isn't my Life Skills teacher. My teacher is Ms. Beach. I've never seen that woman in my life before."

"Oh, really?" Primo whispered, batting his eyes at her. "How interesting. But she looked awfully nice to me, and she was *so* well spoken. Reminded me of Mother, sort of."

She felt his body shaking in his arms. The little guy was chuckling.

"This way, please," said the hefty female deputy sheriff, the one whose job it was to latch on to sentenced female criminals and escort them to the county jail.

Orel and Bunny Sachs were approached by a reporter as they left the courtroom. The young woman must have done her homework, because she knew exactly who they were.

"Hi there, Mr. and Mrs. Sachs," she said perkily. "I'm Brenda Diggs, star reporter with the *Converse Tribune*. Would you give me your reaction to your niece's sentencing? Specifically, how do you feel about her being locked up with adult offenders in the county jail? Are you at all anxious about her safety and well-being while under state supervision?"

Aunt Bunny had anticipated something like this happening, and so, that very morning, she'd been on the phone with Bentley Royce, one of the law partners at Hyde Royce Pommery Hatch, and he had faxed her the statement she now extracted from her purse.

"Mr. Sachs and I," she read, "speaking on behalf of Ann's parents and ourselves, very much regret the poor judgment on this young woman's part that made these proceedings necessary. Ann is immature and headstrong but not, in our opinion, a 'bad' person. She knows that what she did was very wrong and merited the sentence that the court, in its wisdom, imposed. We are confident she will learn her lesson in the next few days and will be a better person for having done so. Thank you very much."

"But don't you think," Ms. Diggs persisted, "that a young girl—a juvenile, as defined by law—may actually be *damaged*, psychologically if not physically, by being locked up with hardened, older criminals?"

"We have no further comment," Aunt Bunny said.

"Since when is punishment not meant to hurt?" exploded

out of Uncle Orel's mouth before Aunt Bunny could get him headed toward their car. "A few good sessions in the woodshed would help these kids stay *out* of trouble, *I* say."

"Looking on the bright side," Aunt Bunny said on the way home, "Fleur will have her guest room back. And hopefully, Ann can be reformed—re-formed—in such a way that she becomes a more responsible young woman. God knows her mother doesn't like advice from me, but there's a place for kids like Ann I've read about—a place other than the county jail, that is—where she might go when she's released from custody and be with other kids from . . . her side of the tracks. It's called 'Back to Basics Center,' and it's in one of those states"—she gestured with one hand, fluttering her fingers—"way out there, in a pleasant rural setting. There, young clients lead a simple, disciplined existence, removed from all temptations and distractions, and soon see the error of their former ways. I'm getting them to send the Irelands their literature, not mentioning my name, of course. Maybe, for once, they'll take some good advice."

Annie and Arby were transported in a van to the county jail, which was just a couple of blocks from the county courthouse. Two sheriff's deputies rode with them—one of the ones who'd taken Arby from the courtroom, and Annie's bulky escort. The Roach Boy was already in the van when Annie, carrying Primo, and her custodian clambered in.

"Oh, Arby," Annie said when she saw her friend, "you

shouldn't have. I mean, I really appreciate what you said and all, but now you're going to jail on my account."

"Hey," said Arby bravely, "I don't mind. I'm sort of used to being locked up, don't forget. And if there're roaches in my cell, I'll probably know some relatives of theirs, from down at the Fright Factory."

That caused Jasper Ochs, the fat-cheeked sheriff's deputy with the Fu Manchu mustache, to look over at him.

"Jeezum," he said. "Don't tell me you're the Roach Boy!"

"I certainly am," said Arby.

"My kid's the biggest fan of yours!" he said. "Halloween, last year, you were all she talked about, seein' all those roaches crawlin' all over you and you just layin' there. 'Ee-yew!' she went, 'that kid is somepin' else! I dunno how he does it!'"

"Oh," said Arby modestly, "it's not that hard to do. They don't bite or anything. And with what I get to wear, they can't crawl into any of my . . . orifices."

"Look," said Deputy Ochs, reaching into his bulging shirt pocket. "D'you think you could gimme an autograph to take to her? All I got's my book of tickets, but there's space up on the top, where you could write. You'd be doing a little girl a mega-favor, man. I swear, this here would make her *year!*"

He handed Arby his best pen, a souvenir from the local feed store.

"Sure," the Roach Boy said. "Be happy to help."

"If you could make it out to Peggy-Sue," Ochs said, "that's P-E-G-G-I dash S-O-O, that'd be terrific. And then sign your real name with 'The Roach Boy' after."

"You got it," Arby said as he started writing.

"And I'll do you a favor in return," the deputy continued. "I'll have a word with the officers down at the jail. They'll take good care of you and—how about it, Marge?—your friend here, too."

"Why not?" said Marge, the female deputy. "No skin off my behind."

Although she'd never visited a real-life jail, Annie had a small idea of what one would be like inside. She'd seen movies, after all, movies in which people (usually guys) were pushed into dingy-looking cells and a big barred door was slammed shut behind them. So she assumed that was the way she and Arby would end up after first being made to change, probably into striped prison uniforms that'd be many sizes too big for them.

But instead of being "processed" right away, they were led into a large, cheerful room with wall-to-wall carpeting that contained a three-seater sofa, several big recliners pointed at a supersize TV, two square wooden tables with molded plastic chairs around them, and against one wall, vending machines filled with all kinds of snacks and sodas.

The room, which turned out to be the deputies' lounge, was also full of people, none of whom were sitting down. The sheriff himself was there, in a uniform that looked brand-new, along with a number of uniformed deputies, several men in suits and eye-catching neckties, a TV cameraman and his associate (who held a microphone), a fellow with a flash camera, and two young women holding pens and pads of paper.

The sheriff, with his broad-brimmed hat clasped under his left arm, stepped toward Annie with a smile on his face and his right hand extended. "Ann Ireland," he said as they shook, "welcome to the Converse County Jail. We've taken the time to run your conviction and sentencing through our computer, and as we hoped might be the case, we've been able to ascertain that you are about to have the distinction of becoming the two millionth prisoner in these United States!"

A flashbulb popped, and the deputies and the suits applauded. The man with the microphone stuck it in front of Annie's face. She realized she was expected to say something, but she wasn't sure that she wanted to. She looked down at Primo. His chin went up and down, almost imperceptibly.

"I'm just wondering," she said, "what the rest of the world will think when it learns that the two millionth prisoner in the land of the free and the home of the brave is a fifteen-year-old girl whose only crime was to write a funny story that her teacher thought was good enough to appear in her high school's literary magazine."

The sheriff's face reddened. "Just for the record," he began, "let me ask you this: Did you not, in your story, have a young female high school student aim and fire at both her teacher and a fellow student, killing the two of them? And isn't it a fact that your imaginary student went scot-free and never suffered any negative consequences from what she did?'

"Well, yes," said Annie, "but—"

"No 'but's,'" the sheriff said, taking Annie by the elbow and propelling her toward the door. "It's time all you kids learned that, in the *real* world, people who mess up go down. And you messed up, big time."

Because Arby was prisoner number two million and one, he was put away with no ceremony whatsoever. The boy was just another convict, presumably paying his debt to society.

12

Conversations and Confusions in the Converse County Jail

There were men's and women's sections in the Converse County Jail, and that meant Arby didn't see Annie and Primo at all while sucking on his five-day sentence. And when the three of them got together afterward and talked about their time as guests of the county, it was clear that Arby'd had the worst of it, in terms of how he'd felt during those 120 hours. By any standard, male inmates tend to be more dangerous than female inmates, and therefore more threatening to an inexperienced teenager. And, of course, Annie and Primo had had each other's company, not to mention his ability to make changes in the world around him.

In some respects, however, the men's and women's sections of the jail were very similar. Both of them were seriously overcrowded, with two prisoners often occupying space designed for one. Both sections, too, smelled awful, due in equal parts to inmates' habits, prison food, too infrequent shower opportunities, and general anxiety. And in both of them bickering and complaining by the inmates (phrased in the language naughty children use) almost never ceased.

Their keepers, the corrections officers, talked much like the prisoners, peppering their speech with the same all-purpose adjective, a vulgar "-ing" word, which, as it was used, had no meaning other than to tell the world its user didn't give a . . . well, another all-purpose word, a vulgar noun, which, in this usage, also had no meaning other than to tell the world its user didn't care what "nice" people thought of him or her.

"We're runnin' at about a hundred and sixty-four percent of capacity," guard Eldon Beadle told Arby when the boy had walked into the men's section of the jail—and shuddered when the locked door slammed shut behind him. "So we got eighteen guys sleepin' in the [all-purpose vulgar adjective] gym. I've had to assign you an upper bed on one of the double-deckers there, but you'll ackshually be sleepin' on the [all-purpose vulgar adjective] floor, there in the guards' office, just like I promised Deputy Ochs you would. I'll get you a [all-purpose vulgar adjective] inflatable mattress. It won't be too bad."

"Yes, sir. Fine. I thank you," Arby said. He considered adding, *That's awfully [all-purpose vulgar adjective] nice of you*, but he decided against it.

The other prisoners hanging around in the gym pretty much ignored his arrival. They were mostly young, but he was the only inmate in the room who didn't have long sideburns.

•••

"[All-purpose vulgar noun]! You're just a [all-purpose vulgar adjective] kid!" said the skinny older inmate with the really bad teeth and the scar running from one corner of his mouth to just below his ear.

"Yep, I guess I am," said Arby, avoiding eye contact with the man but not wanting to be rude. He was walking rapid laps around the exercise yard, the morning of his second day, wearing his XL county-issue orange jumpsuit. The other inmates were lifting weights, or playing volleyball or half-court basketball, or watching the men who were doing those things. The skinny older inmate had been sitting on a bench watching the basketball until he'd seen Arby walk by. Then he'd gotten up and walked fast till he caught up with him.

"You ain't been in a place like this before, I bet," the inmate said. Arby thought he looked like someone who could have spent a lot of time in places very much like this.

"No," said Arby. "That's correct. I haven't."

"Well, it's a [all-purpose vulgar adjective] zoo," the inmate said, "but I'll look after you. You hang around with me, and nobody'll [all-purpose vulgar adjective] touch you, okay?"

Arby felt his heart speed up. Of course, he didn't know for sure exactly what the man had in mind when he said "look after you" and "hang around with me," but he'd heard enough prison horror stories to have a pretty good idea of what "[all-purpose vulgar adjective] touch you" meant.

He scoured his mind for something he could say. Something *tough* or *ugly* hopefully, something that'd send this guy a message, suggest to him that he wasn't what he really was, some helpless little pigeon.

"No offense, mister," he began, "but my uncle told me not to hang around with nobody in here. My uncle Nick—who owns the Fright Factory, along with various other establishments?"

He had no idea if this man would have ever heard of his uncle, but his mother'd told him once that her brother had "big-time connections" (and she'd rolled her eyes around) and was a man that "no one ever messed with, ever."

"[All-purpose vulgar noun]!" the man exclaimed, and he stopped walking. "You're Nicky Nosebleed's [all-purpose vulgar adjective] nephew? I bet you think you're real hot stuff, you little [all-purpose vulgar noun]." And mumbling to himself, he went back to his seat by the basketball game.

The next time Arby came around the yard, a number of the basketball spectators looked over at him, kind of took him in, with what he actually thought could be *respect*.

"What none of these [all-purpose vulgar adjective] morons seem to understand," said the inmate sitting across from Arby at lunch, two days later, "is that computers are already running the whole [all-purpose vulgar adjective] country. A big computer can think a hundred times faster than the human brain, so it can use the person who thinks he's using it, even big-shot scientists. I heard all about it on my radio. There's this one station that the [all-purpose vulgar adjective] Unabomber broad-

casts from. He's the one guy that's even smarter than computers, and he broadcasts from the prison where they've got
him, just using his [all-purpose vulgar adjective] brain waves.
Maybe you can pick him up, if you go all the way to the right
on your radio dial, the same as I do. All these [all-purpose vulgar adjective] guys around here are too damn ignorant to—"

"Wallace, will you shut your [all-purpose vulgar adjective]
hole? And let the kid eat his lunch in peace?" said the prisoner
on Arby's left.

"Don't pay him any mind," the man then said to Arb. "He's
[all-purpose vulgar adjective] crazy. Everybody knows that for a
fact, 'cept for him and the stupid [all-purpose vulgar adjective]
judge who put him in here. He tried to kill a cable TV guy he
thought was buggin' his apartment."

"I see," said Arby, staring at his dry bologna sandwich.

"You got no need to be afraid of Tish there, honey," guard
Jermaine "Jay" Walker said to Annie, her first day. "She big,
but she a sweetheart." The guard nodded in the direction of a
nineteen-year-old, 250-pound inmate with high coloring and
a long braid down her back. "The other ladies here don't mess
with her," she added. "A lot of them, they wish they had the
guts to do what she done."

"What'd she do?" asked Annie. The corrections officer was
almost as big as the inmate Tish, and she'd taken Annie under
her wing, promising to tell her "what was what." She'd already
said it was "plain-ass wrong" for them to put "a sweet young

lady like yourself" in county jail. Annie was amazed to realize that this woman, who she'd only just met, already liked her better than her aunt Bunny did.

"Shot her boyfriend," said the guard. "Big ol' boy named Roly-Poly Foley. Maybe you read about it? Tried to blow his [all-purpose vulgar adjective] head off. Served him [all-purpose vulgar adjective] right, from what I heard."

"Your baby's just as cute as them new CK panties," said the inmate Tish as she handed Pantagruel Primo, Esquire, back to Annie.

"Well, thank you," Annie said. "*I* sure think he is." She was very glad that Primo, now recumbent on her lap, didn't have the power to pinch.

"I wanta have a baby," said the large young woman, "but it's gotta be with the right fella, you know what I mean? Not some jerk like that [all-purpose vulgar adjective] Roly. You ever been to Disneyworld? That's where I went after I did Roly; I spent all his [all-purpose vulgar adjective] money down there. I wish I coulda stayed in Florida. It's real nice, like, lotsa stuff to do. Here, it's [all-purpose vulgar adjective] boring, don't you think?"

Annie didn't know how she ought to answer that, so she just shrugged. The truth was, she hadn't found jail boring at all. Although the guards and this big girl were being really nice to her, this was still *jail*. She was surrounded by strangers, any of whom could beat her up, if they happened to feel like it, and some of whom, from what she'd overheard, often felt like doing exactly that, sometimes just for the fun of it.

"And besides, it [all-purpose vulgar adjective] *stinks* in here," Tish continued. "You kinda get used to it after a while, but then you come in from the yard and it just about knocks you over. You musta noticed it, the first time you walked in."

"Well, yeah, it is a little . . . gamey," Annie said.

"*Gamey?* It's [all-purpose vulgar adjective] *disgusting*," Tish opined. "They oughta *do* something about it; that's what *I* think."

"That behemoth Tish is right, you know," Primo whispered to Annie when they got into bed that night. "Something *should* be done about the stench in here." The two of them occupied a cot that had been set up in the walkway outside the row of cells. The guard on duty could (and would, she told Annie) keep an eye on her all night.

"I can't imagine what anyone *could* do," said Annie, "short of putting liquefied deodorant in the sprinkler system."

"Oh, I don't know," said Primo. "Just think: The thing that makes it smell so fresh and clean outside is *nature*—all those trees and shrubs and flowers, even meadow grasses, all exhaling their delightful scents."

"Yeah, right," said Annie. "But there's no way that can happen here. I don't see any flowerpots or planters in this place. How could *anything* grow in here—except for fungus, maybe?"

"Well," said Primo—and Annie knew, just from the way he said the word, that he was up to something. "There's always *hydroponics*."

The words had hardly left his mouth before a veritable uproar—curses, screams, and shouts—erupted in the cell block. "Oh, my God!" and "Holy [all-purpose vulgar noun]!" were two popular choices, but an inmate by the name of Sherry Sekko went into specific detail.

"Ow! What the hell?" she yelled. "There's an *alligator* in my [all-purpose vulgar adjective] toilet! It just bit me on my [all-purpose vulgar adjective] butt!"

Reacting to the inmates' cries, the night guard switched the dimmed lights back to their full brightness, and Annie, who'd gotten out of bed in a bit of a panic, could now see the cause of all the excitement. Looming out of every toilet in the cell block (there was one in every cell) was not an amphibious reptile, but a growing, flowering plant, or bush, or little tree.

She turned and looked at Primo. He was lying on his side and had his eyes closed, feigning sleep—and innocence. She realized this was just the sort of trick a little person (like himself) would love to play.

Meanwhile, all the inmates in the cells had also gotten out of bed and were calling to one another and the officer on duty, many of them laughing now and sniffing at the flowers that had so suddenly popped up in their living quarters. Sherry Sekko, the inmate who'd been sitting on her toilet, was standing looking at the purple lilac growing from it now. She'd been lucky, actually: The next cell down the line now held a handsome (though real thorny) rosebush.

The officer on duty was confounded and perplexed. Inmates were not permitted plants (or pets) inside their cells; a rule was being broken. But how all the inmates had managed to smuggle in these good-size nursery items she could not imagine.

"All right, ladies, that's enough," she cried, trying to make herself heard above the din. "Maintenance will be here in the morning. All your [all-purpose vulgar adjective] shrubbery has got to go. Them toilets in your cells is there for sanitary purposes only."

The next morning, when a work crew from maintenance arrived at the cell block, there wasn't any vegetation visible in any of the cells. The officer who'd been in charge was accused of drinking while on duty and was ordered to undergo counseling.

And for the rest of the day the atmosphere in the cell block was noticeably better: fresher, cleaner, even lightly scented. And each and every one of the inmates maintained that she'd had "this incredible [all-purpose vulgar adjective] dream."

13.

Sprung

In a concession to the ages of his two youngest prisoners ever, the sheriff of Converse County had telephoned Annie Ireland's parents and Nemo Skank's mother and told them they could come and pick up their kids at 3:00 P.M. the day their sentences were up. So, when Annie and Arby, newly reunited with their shoelaces and other personal possessions, exited the jail, there stood Patrick and Eileen Ireland, along with Gloria Skank and her brother, Nicholas Stiletto (aka "Nick Nix" as well as "Nicky Nosebleed"). Arby's father, Justin Skank, may have been there too, in spirit; his Ford Escort had been brushed out of its way by an SUV, fatally for him, five years before.

Although her father had indeed lost weight (some $47,000 worth), Annie had no trouble recognizing either him or her mother. And that was in spite of the fact that the two of them were dressed in brand-new clothes, quite different from the ones they'd left town in.

Patrick Ireland had started looking like an overweight

hound dog in his senior year in college, when a diet high in beer and double-cheese-on-everything had added to his jowls and made his eyes a little bloodshot and regretful. His "look" used to be dark suits or, oftentimes, well-tailored slacks and sports coats. Now he was wearing narrow, faded Levi's and a polo shirt (by Polo) and black snakeskin cowboy boots. By making him two inches taller, they also made him seem more slender, he believed.

His wife, Eileen, still had the good-looking legs (which Annie had inherited) and the over-the-top personality that had helped her to be chosen head cheerleader at her high school, but her torso had become less of an excitement over the years, and her free-swinging hair had been tamed and curled and organized by a genius named Ricardo at the Hair Apparent. Annie guessed her mom had done less well at Negative Feedback than her father had because she had on a floor-length, orange-patterned muu-muu, worn with white buckle thong sandals under glossy reddish-orange painted toenails.

Arby's mother, Gloria, and her brother, Nick, were dressed about the same as they had been for years, she by The Bon-Ton over in Coldbrook, he by Maraschino Brothers of Miami.

"My poor sweetie! You okay?" Gloria ran toward Arby, wrapped him in a hug. "I can't imagine what that judge was thinking of, sending you to jail. Just for sticking up for Annie. The county jail is no place for a boy your age. Everybody's furious about this."

"How you doin', kid?" Uncle Nick asked Arby when he'd

disengaged himself from his adoring mom. "Nobody messed wit' you or nuttin', right?"

"No, I'm fine. *Really*, Mom. Everyone was nice to me," said Arby. "But I'm sure glad to be out. It's pretty . . . not so nice in there."

Meanwhile, Annie had also gotten hugs from both her parents, which had felt a little "by the book," she thought.

"I bet you're glad that's over with," her father said. "I can't tell you what a shock it was to us when your aunt Bunny called. If there'd been anything we could have done to help, we would have rushed right back. But from what she said, the judge believed he had to send a message—mostly to the kids in Converse County."

"Of course, we think he overreacted," Annie's mother said. "Jail is no place for a girl your age. Granted, it was a little thoughtless of you to write a story like that—though both your father and I *liked* it, as a piece of writing. You have a wonderful imagination, dear. I think you get that from my dad. He could tell the greatest stories."

"At this point we're just glad we can put the whole thing behind us," her father said. "I don't think this little . . . bump in the road ought to cause any of us to lose sleep, or friends. 'Most everyone we know has been supportive. Mrs. Reynolds even sent your mother flowers."

"Yes," Eileen Ireland chimed in. "As she well knows, we aren't the first parents who've had a son's or daughter's troubles get into the papers. People forgive and forget, though. Everyone needs friends. Already, people have made a point of telling me how great your father looks."

Annie wasn't sure what she'd expected from her parents. She'd had too many other things on her mind to worry about what their reaction to . . . well, *everything* would be. She'd been almost relieved when Aunt Bunny told her they wouldn't be able to make it to the trial. Probably, she just assumed they'd see how totally absurd it had been to charge her with *anything*. Aunt Bunny and (especially) Uncle Orel hadn't seemed to see that, but they were just her aunt and uncle, not her parents.

What she was feeling now was not surprise; her parents often talked about how the things that *she* did affected *them*. Nor was it simply disappointment. It was different, also more complex, than simple disappointment. Up to this point she'd always felt that her parents, although certainly critical, would always be there for her, that she'd always be (as her father liked to say) their "little girl."

But now it seemed she wasn't "little" anymore and so was no longer entitled to their sticking-up-for, in any and all cir-cumstances. Because she'd been "thoughtless" enough to write that story and had (therefore) been sentenced by a judge to jail time and had gotten the Ireland name in the paper, she'd been moved a little way out of the nest and put much more on her own than she had been before.

Well, so be it, she thought. Her new status was a little scary but a little thrilling, too. She remembered what Primo'd said about everybody having their own things they were good at and how that made them unique. He'd implied that it was natural and good for her to see herself as separate from, unlike, her parents.

Maybe, she thought, *maybe I* am *a very different person.* And maybe that was fine and inevitable and something that she shouldn't want to change. Maybe that was one of Primo's Forget-About-Its. Maybe she should try to stop worrying about whether she was pleasing her parents or not; maybe that shouldn't be one of the main purposes of her life.

Even as she thought those thoughts, she heard her mother speaking—to her, but also seemingly to Arby and his mother and his uncle.

"So, now we're all faced with the question of what's next," she was saying. "How would it be for these kids if they went back to Converse High? What kind of a reception would they get, from teachers and from fellow students?"

"Why wouldn't it be a good one?" Annie asked. "I didn't do anything wrong. All I did was write a story. That was our assignment: to write a story on an assigned topic, 'Life's Darkest Moment,' and to use our imaginations. My English teacher liked my story so much, she put it in the school's literary magazine. Everybody knows that." Annie found she was getting really sick of telling the story of her story. "And Arby didn't do anything but tell the judge he was wrong to punish me."

"Maybe so," said her father. "But that doesn't mean your story didn't touch a nerve in the larger community. Good God, girl—you were sentenced by a well-respected judge; you were put into the county jail. If you went back to Converse High, you and Nemo here would be the only ex-convicts in the entire school. You can't tell me that some kids—and teachers—might not be bothered by having jailbirds in their classes. You can't tell me that your presence in the school might not cause reactions—unfavorable reactions, maybe even hostile ones."

Arby had been listening to this entire conversation—his mother and his uncle, too—and now, because his name had been brought into it, he felt he was entitled to contribute.

"Oh, I don't think anybody'd have a problem, Mr. Ireland. Annie has a lot of friends at school, and so do I," he said. "I'm not saying we're the most popular kids in our class or anything like that, but we get along with just about everyone. And kids don't always side with the grown-up who's in charge—like the principal or this judge. I think kids are mostly into fairness."

"Well, that's very nice, dear," Eileen Ireland said. She'd never been completely crazy about Arby; she thought her daughter could do better, friendshipwise. "But there's no way you could know what older people in town have been thinking and saying. After all, you've been in jail the last five days. I'm not going to tell you every single soul is going to condemn or ostracize you two, but you know as well as I do that people old *and* young can be very mean at times. The two of you are only freshmen, and there are a lot of older kids in that school who may have all sorts of . . . prejudices. You don't know what they're hearing at home and what sort of reactions their parents may be seeming to encourage. Maybe they believe that you've disgraced *their* school."

That was too much for Arby's mother to ignore.

"You don't really think there's any *danger* if the kids go back to school, do you?" she asked the Irelands. "*My* neighbors have all said they were furious at that judge for putting Nemo and Annie in jail."

"And nobody's said nuttin' bad about the kid to me," Arby's uncle Nick put in. Then he seemed to think that over. "Not that they'd be apt to, probably," he added.

"Well, we're just not willing to take a chance of something . . . unfortunate happening," said Patrick Ireland. "I've gotten in touch with a Dr. Smithers, who's director of a school that's called the 'Back to Basics Center.' It's out of state, in a lovely remote rural area, and it's in business to serve families like ours—and kids like Annie and Nemo who've gotten themselves in some kind of trouble. I understand that they've got a good track record and that the kids who've been there come away with a whole new outlook on life."

"What?" said Annie. "You're talking about sending me to a boarding school? I don't want to go to any boarding school. I like it here; I want to stay with my friends. I want to live in our new house as soon as it's finished and get back to living my old life, before all this . . . stuff happened. I don't think I *need* 'a whole new outlook.'"

Pantagruel Primo, Esquire, had been lying quietly in Annie's arms ever since they emerged from the jail, but now she felt his head go up and down, nodding in emphatic agreement.

"We can talk about all this when we get home, dear," Annie's mother said. "All we want is to be on the safe side." She turned to Arby's mom and uncle with a cheery smile and added, "We've rented a house up in the Notch, while we rebuild."

"I'm sure the more you think about it," she said, turning back to Annie, "the more you'll see we're right."

"Could you give me the number of this Dr. Smithers guy?" Arby's uncle Nick said suddenly. "Maybe we should look into this Back to Basics place for Nemo. Just to be, like you said, on the safe side. What the hell"—he chuckled—"basics is good; you gotta have the basics. And lots of classy kids go off to private school."

"Absolutely," Annie's father said, agreeing. He took one of his own business cards out of his wallet and scribbled on the back of it. "I've got the number up there memorized, I've called it that much. This Smithers sounds like a very capable fellow. By all means, use my name if you want to, when you talk to him. Maybe they'll give us a two-for-one deal on the tuition, if you decide to send Nemo." And *he* chuckled at his little joke. "For what they charge, their program must be good!"

Annie looked at Arby. Five days in jail had been bad enough, and now their families were talking about maybe shipping them off to some weirdo boarding school? She'd known kids who'd gone away to prep schools, but their schools all had one-word names or saints' names, not at all like the Back to Basics Center. Both of their reactions were the same: unthinkable!

"I'll call you," she told him as the families began to go their separate ways. *Thank God it's Friday,* she was thinking. They'd have the weekend to construct a strong rebuttal to this whole absurd idea.

14.

Meeting Brad and Sophie

"I believe they're deadly serious," said Annie. "I can tell. As soon as they start hitting me with 'When you've been on the planet half as long as we have . . . ,' I know it's time to circle the wagons."

"Yeah—know whatcha mean," said Arby, with his mouth full.

It was close to noon on Saturday. They were out on the deck that ran along the back of the Skanks' modest bungalow, slouched in a couple of the white plastic chairs that were grouped around a white tin table that had once had an umbrella coming out its middle. Before he'd hung up the phone, Arby had asked his mom if she'd pick up Annie and bring her down to their house before she headed to the mall, and she'd said yes. For their first meal of the day the kids had rooted around in Gloria's kitchen cabinets and pulled out a box of orange-glazed donuts and a bag of nacho-cheesier tortilla chips. Then they'd popped the tops off bright green cans of Mountain Dew.

Primo, who'd ridden down with Annie, was sitting stiff-legged in a chair of his own. So far, he'd kept his opinion of their breakfast choices to himself.

"It's like Uncle Nick now has this *thing* for private school," Arby went on, having sent his mouthful sliding south, diluted by a slurp of Dew. "I swear, he'd never mentioned it before, but now he's like a salesman for the darn things. He says they're all about contacts, about getting in with the right people. 'You go to private school,' he says, 'you're in the fat cats' club.'"

"My parents haven't said *that*," said Annie. "They just keep insisting that they know 'a change of scenery' will do me good. They say that now they're glad *their* parents made them do some stuff they didn't want to do."

"But your parents wouldn't try to *make* you go to a school you didn't want to go to, would they?" Primo asked. His eyes went back and forth from Annie to Arby and then back to Annie again.

"No," said Arby flatly.

"I don't think so," Annie said, sounding a good deal less certain.

"D'you suppose the people running a school would take a kid who really didn't want to go to it?" asked Arby. "I wouldn't think so. They'd know the kid would run away or be a pain in the ass to have around. If our parents talk us into visiting this Basics place, all we'd have to do is tell the principal to shove it."

"Right. All the kids I know who went away to school this year *wanted* to go," said Annie. "Or at least they acted like they did." She put on a namby-pamby voice, "*I'm* going to Exeter, while you're still stuck in this dumb hole."

"Well, I'm not sure I want to go away either," said Primo. "Slurpagar assigned me to a baby's body in the town of Converse. He's not the brightest flash of lightning in the evening sky. Suppose he realized one fine day that he'd gotten his revenge and that the spell he'd put on me wasn't funny anymore. And so then he went looking for me to take it off but couldn't find me—because I was stuck in some repulsively remote rural area, where you two were supposedly polishing up your basics. That'd be calamitous, to say the least."

"Me and Annie don't need work on any basics," Arby said "Annie and I can do long division standing on our heads. Want to hear me sound out unfamiliar words?"

"Well then, we're all agreed?' said Annie. "It's 'Hell no, we won't go'?"

"That's my position," Arby said.

"Felicitously phrased," said Primo.

Somewhat after midnight, which made it more than twelve hours after the "Hell no, we won't go" agreement, Annie was fast asleep and having a dream in which she was trying to put up the family Christmas tree and having a hard time of it. Over and over, she kept jamming it into this amusing new stand her mother'd bought, which was made in the shape of a toilet.

"Just shove it in there," her mother was saying. "Come on. Let's go."

And then she was awake and someone was jiggling her shoulder, saying, "Annie! Hey, wake up. Come on, let's go. You've got to hurry."

And when her eyes were open, "Hi, I'm Sophie."

A light was on, so she could see this Sophie person pretty clearly. She thought she looked . . . okay, like an all-American college girl (better make that "graduate"). She had blond hair, cut in a pageboy bob, but her baby face had started to attract the lines of early middle age. She wore no discernible makeup and but a single gold chain around her neck. Her clothes were country casual, the sort of stuff that L.L. Bean would sell you to wear on a camping trip but that would still not get you dirty looks in a Mercedes showroom.

"What's happening?" said Annie. Although technically awake, she couldn't think straight yet. "Is the house on fire? Not again! How'd you get in here, anyway?"

"I'm friends with your parents," Sophie said. "They're right downstairs. They sent me up. Come on, let's hurry now. Get dressed."

Annie got up, shaking her head. What was happening did not make any sense. She staggered out into the hall. There were lights on downstairs, and she heard voices, her parents' and a man's.

"Mom? Dad?" she called. "What's going on? It's the middle of the night. How come you're up?"

Her father answered. "It's okay," he said. "You'll see. Just get dressed and come on down. Don't dawdle, honey."

Annie'd gone to bed in a T-shirt and underpants, so she left them on and added jeans, a long-sleeved shirt, and running shoes and socks.

She could feel Sophie watching her as she got dressed. On second look, she'd decided Sophie could be a soccer coach, a young phys ed teacher. That had to do with the way she stood there, grinning, feet shoulder width apart, balanced on her lightweight hiking boots, arms crossed under authoritative breasts.

What Sophie *didn't* look like was what she'd said she was: "friends with your parents." Her parents didn't have any "friends" who were Sophie's age—or had anything to do with organized athletics. Annie wondered if Sophie could possibly be a personal trainer whom they met out at Negative Feedback and talked into working for them. Maybe Sophie was going to personally train *her* too, and that was why her parents wanted them to meet. But in the middle of the night?

Whatever was going on, though, Annie wanted Pantagruel Primo to observe it and, later, give her his opinion. In a very short time he'd become more than just an unbelievable *something* with powers right out of a Harry Potter book. He was also, she believed, quite *wise*—a word that up until now she'd heard only at Christmastime, after "three" and before "men," and had used only when she was picking out potato chips. So, when she was fully dressed, she went and snatched him up before she left the room. She didn't care what Sophie thought of that, of someone her age picking up a doll. And she thought *he* looked . . . alarmed.

In the living room downstairs her parents had empty mugs in front of them on the coffee table, and they were dressed the same as they had been when she went up to bed. Those things made Sherlock Annie think they'd known someone was coming and had waited up. They'd waited up for Sophie and . . . another stranger, who stood up when she arrived.

"And this is *Brad*," her mother said, bearing down on his name—coyly, Annie thought, as if to say, *Now, don't you think he's* cute?

Brad *was* good-looking, in a seventeenth-century bad-boy sort of way, Annie thought. She could imagine him in one of those Queen Elizabeth movies, playing a young Spanish duke, the one with the droopy mustache and the black goatee, the one with hooded, scheming eyes. His present costume wasn't right for the part, though: jeans and hiking boots and a windbreaker, with a well-worn narrow-brimmed cowboy hat under one arm.

"Hi, Annie," Brad said casually. And then to her parents, "We really oughta get going, Mr. and Mrs. Ireland." He stuck out a hand for them to shake.

Annie started to relax. The company was leaving. But then she stopped relaxing. Why had she been gotten up, been told to dress? Just so this Brad could see her?

Then she became aware of something new. Sophie was right next to her; their hips were touching. And Sophie's hand was on her back.

"Come on, Annie," Sophie said, putting on a little pressure, trying to move her toward the hall, and the front door.

"Hey, cut it out. What's happening?" Annie aimed the question at her parents. "I'm not going anywhere."

"Brad and Sophie are counselors at the Back to Basics Center," Mr. Ireland said. He chuckled. "Or the 'BBC,' as they like to say. They were in the area and were nice enough to offer you a ride up there, so you could see the place and give it a try."

"So I could see the Back to Basics Center?" Annie said. "But I don't want to do that, Dad. I don't want to go there—ever."

"Well, actually," her mother said, "we took the liberty of making the decision for you—the decision to go, that is. It's for your own good, dearie. Brad and Sophie think you'll fit in perfectly; we've told them all about you. I'm sure you'll like them when you get to know them. We think they're really, really nice." She simpered at the two of them.

"You mean I have to go with them *right now*, in the middle of the night?" said Annie. She could feel herself getting upset, getting really fractured, even more upset than when she'd learned she'd have to go to jail. For that, there'd been (at least) an explanation—and jail was for five days, no more than that, right there in town.

"You're *making* me do this?" she almost screamed.

"Let's not put it that way," said her father. "This is something that you're going to thank us for someday, you'll see. So go along with Brad and Sophie like a good girl, now. As your mother said, they're really nice, fun people. And after you've given the BBC a good try, we can all get together and decide how long you ought to stay."

"Didn't you hear what I said?" said Annie, and she was starting to cry. "I don't want to go *at all*. I want to stay right here with you!" She knew that sounded babyish, but she didn't care.

She made a sudden turn, away from Sophie, but before she could create real space between them, strong fingers had her by the arm, and Brad had gotten to her other side and had *that* arm, and two hands had slid around her waist, one from each side.

"It's time to go now, kid," Brad said quietly. She'd had a riding instructor when she was little who'd talked to horses in that tone of voice. "You're going to come with us, so why not make it easy on yourself? Like your parents said, we're really nice. But we're also real determined. We're leaving here right now, and you're going with us to the center. That's all she wrote and end of story."

15.

In the Van

They had a van. It was specially equipped, in much the same way a lot of police cars are. There was a clear plastic shield behind the front bucket seats to keep the people up there from being bonked from behind. In the back there were no inside doors or window handles, and the glass was extra thick and tinted so that no one could see in. From the carpet on the floor there came, thanks to a former passenger, a whiff of puke.

She didn't want to cry. She didn't want those two to think she was intimidated, weak, a pushover. But she was furious as well as scared, and she was finding out that when she got this angry, it was very hard not to cry. Her parents had betrayed her; they'd handed her over to this pair, totally against her will. Here she was, fifteen, well beyond the age where parents decide everything important, no discussion. But they'd decided something huge: to just *get rid of her*. It was as simple as that. *How could they?*

She thought she hated them. *How could she not?*

She also hated Brad and Sophie. She swallowed twice and cleared her throat.

"This is illegal, you know," she croaked at the backs of their heads. She would have given anything to sound *tough*. "You've kidnapped me. And if you take me across a state line, it'll be a federal offense. The FBI'll be coming after you someday. You can't get away with this. You'll be in jail a long, long time."

"Wrong," said Sophie calmly. "Your parents signed you over. For now, the center is your guardian. You have no legal rights at your age. So, like they say, tough noogies, kid." And she giggled.

Annie gulped. Could that be right—that she now belonged (almost) to Brad and Sophie and to that Dr. Smithers (was it?), the guy her father'd talked to at the center?

But then she thought that there was something she could do, legal rights or no legal rights. As Arby'd said, a school wouldn't want to have to deal with a kid who really didn't want to go to it. Maybe she could make *them* hate *her*—so much so that they'd want to ship her back to Converse.

"Well, maybe I'll just run away," she said. "And before I do, I'll be a real pain in the butt. I won't do anything you tell me to do."

Saying that made her feel strange. She'd never talked like that to someone older. Maybe she'd wanted to, at times, but she never had; she'd always been a "good girl." This was sort of like trying to get comfortable in clothes that were completely different from the kind you were used to wearing. Or getting used to a tongue stud, maybe.

"A lot of people woof like that at first," said Brad. He sounded more bored than apprehensive. "You'll change your tune. Everybody does. If you run away, you won't get far. No one ever has. After a while you'll turn into a little pussycat. How long that takes is strictly up to you."

"It'll all depend on how much you want to graduate," added Sophie. "You can have a really lousy time at the center, but you don't have to. Like Brad just said, it's up to you."

"And now," said Brad, "we have this other stop to make. You're gonna have some company back there."

Annie stared out the window. They were pulling up in front of Arby's house.

She hadn't been thinking about Arby, about the possibility that Arby's mom—and especially his uncle, who'd be the one to pay for it—had decided to send him to the BBC too. She hadn't been thinking about anything but herself and how pissed off and miserable she was.

So now—she was pretty sure her friend was in for it, the same as she was—she found herself reacting in two different ways, almost at once. At first, she thought: *Poor Arby!* And then: *I'm glad he's coming with me; now I won't be all alone up there.*

She was a bit ashamed of that second thought, but she couldn't pretend she hadn't had it. And maybe it reminded her that she, in her misery, already *had* company, that she had Primo on her lap.

Brad and Sophie left the van and headed up the walk that led to Arby's front door.

"Well . . . ," said Primo sharply as soon as the two were gone. "*This* is a fine state of affairs, I *must* say." His tone of voice wasn't exactly the one that Annie wanted to hear just then. He'd sounded just as pissed off as she was, and, if anything, more critical than sympathetic.

"It sure is," she answered, also sharply. "And now we've stopped at Arby's house. It looks as if he's going too."

And at that point another unwelcome thought occurred to her, souring her mood still further.

"Which'll be *my* fault, in a way, I suppose," she said, "seeing that it's *my* stupid story that got him into all this in the first place." She paused. "Or maybe I should say *our* stupid story," she added.

"Oh, no, you don't," said Primo. "It was *your* creation, missy. Who took all the bows when it got published? Not P. Primo, thank you very much. *I* didn't get a byline out of it."

"Well," said Annie, "whoever's work it was doesn't make a whole lot of difference right now. We're all on our way to some stupid 'remote rural area.' Unless, that is, the only one of us who *can*"—she stared at Primo pointedly—"decides to stop this trip from happening."

"I suppose," he said, "that you mean me." He looked uncomfortable.

"Indeed I do," said Annie.

"Perhaps I should feel flattered," Primo said. "But this tone of voice that you've adopted—accusatory, on the one hand, yet expectant, on the other—rather puts me off. And makes me almost glad I have to tell you something."

"Oh, yes?' said Annie snottily. "And that is . . . ?"

"That is the following," said Primo. "Our Mellow Pages—the book of rules to which I alluded earlier—does more than just forbid my people to interfere with any country's laws and their enforcement. There's tons of other stuff that we can't do in there. In fact, we're not allowed to directly overturn *anybody's* orders, judgments, rulings, instructions, decrees, edicts, commandments, directions, decisions, requirements, or regulations."

"*What?*" said Annie. "You're telling me that you can't keep Arby and me from going to this BBC just because our parents decided to send us?"

"Exactly," Primo said quite calmly.

"And that if a Brad or a Sophie tells us to do something, that's it?" she asked, her voice rising in anger and disbelief.

"Well, sort of," Primo said. "You *could* say that."

"So what in the hell *can* you do, you and your people?" Annie cried, now totally disgusted.

"I've told you that before. We can play tricks," he said, "as you have seen."

She thought that over. "You can make worms come out of sandwiches and bushes out of toilets—right. And you changed your friend into a toad once. Very funny, I guess. But how about a trick that's really helpful to somebody? Would you like to show me one of those, right now?"

"No," said Primo. "I'm not in the mood."

"You're not in the mood," repeated Annie slowly. "That's wonderful. Well, I just hope you're in the mood to go to wherever we're going, which I imagine will be a long, long way from where your friend Slurpagar will go looking for you someday . . . you hope."

"I'm not in the mood for that, either," he said. "But let me remind you that I'm going there because you took me with you."

"Okay. Then how'd you like it if I threw you out the door when they open it to shove Arby in?" she said meanly. "That way, you'd stay in Converse and you could stop blaming *me* for everything."

"I wouldn't like that," Primo said quietly.

Annie'd regretted her threat almost as soon as the words were out of her mouth. What sort of person would toss a helpless little being, one trapped inside the body of a school-issue doll, out of a car door and onto the side of a road? Not someone like her, for God's sake. She was a kind, considerate, respectful-of-all-living-things kind of kid. But her wanting to apologize to Primo came crashing up against the mountain of pissed-offedness that had built up inside her, starting at the moment Sophie'd waked her up. So she said nothing.

And at that moment there came Brad and Sophie down the walk with Arby in between them. He was resisting more than she had. Brad had a hold of the back of his pants and was almost lifting him off the ground (while giving him the wedgie to end all wedgies, she assumed), and Sophie had twisted one of his arms way up behind his back.

Seconds later, they'd unloaded him through the van's side door, almost onto Primo, who was still stretched out on Annie's lap.

"You all be good back there," said Brad, adjusting the rear-view mirror as he started the van. "The both of you are now officially enrolled in the BBC and are expected to observe our big long list of no-nos, one of which, I oughta tell you, is: No making out. Except with members of the staff, that is."

And he and Sophie laughed.

16

On the Journey to the BBC

Though Annie had never liked "going for a drive" with her parents, this trip, on less and less well-traveled roads—it lasted for a good twelve hours—was an even less enjoyable experience. Starting with this unpleasant truth: She couldn't believe that what was happening to her was really happening. To put it bluntly, the journey to the BBC, looked at from whatever angle, sucked. For reasons such as these:

• The stops along the way

Twice, they stopped for "chow" (Brad's no-nonsense synonym for what he handed them to eat). Both times, he parked the van away from other cars, a good ways from his quarry, then squared his shoulders and marched off to hunt alone. The items he scored for his two captives were cellophane-wrapped bologna and cheese sandwiches (made at least two real dry days before, by Annie's reckoning), cans of orange soda ("Hey, you

gotta have your vitamin C," he told them), and either gra-
nola bars or pieces of a strangely chemical-tasting carrot cake
("Health food'll keep you regular, amigos"). He and Sophie ate
out of a cooler that they had up front.

Three other times, Annie and Arby were escorted to rest
rooms, the kind that were supposed to be kept locked, so
Sophie and Brad had to get the keys from the service station
guy. Annie thought the ladies' rooms looked as if they'd last
been used by women who'd decided that the service station
guy would have to pay for breaking up with them. Either that
or people unfamiliar with the way that one was meant to use
(or not use) modern plumbing fixtures.

- "The Borborygmi"

Dr. Smithers, the director, had given that name to the
"tribe" that would consist of Annie and Arby and four other
new kids, Brad and Sophie told them. Apparently, all students
at the BBC were grouped in tribes, all of which were named by
Dr. Smithers.

"Dr. Smithers said that your name, Borborygmi, is the plural
of 'borborygmus,'" Sophie told them. "Bet you two don't know
what *that* is." And she giggled.

They said nothing.

"Well then, I'll tell you," Sophie babbled on. "It's that rum-
bling sound you have in your gut sometimes, when you've got
gas."

"In other words, you aren't even little farts yet," chortled Brad, slapping his thigh in celebration of his wit. "But worry not, my dears, you will be."

• Their weaknesses—and the center's corresponding strengths

"You know the trouble with you kids?" asked Sophie rhetorically. She'd just switched off from driving and had turned to look at her counselees, with one arm thrown over her seat back. They could hear her perfectly, in spite of the plastic shield between them. *Unfortunately,* thought Annie.

"You haven't had instilled in you," Sophie went on, "what we at the BBC believe are, like, the twin foundations of a happy, useful, teenage life: structure and discipline. 'S and D,' for short! So it sort of isn't your fault that you behaved so badly. Your parents probably let you do whatever you wanted, which is like giving you sugarcoated junk food to eat instead of good whole grains and lots of different veggies." Sophie's little lecture was delivered in a condescending and self-satisfied tone of voice that she herself believed was "friendly."

"But in a way, it is too their fault," corrected driver Brad. "Other little acne factories whose parents didn't make *them* do what's right didn't screw up half as bad as these two did."

Annie scowled at being called an "acne factory" by Brad. *His* complexion wouldn't win a door prize at the Body Shop, she didn't think. But she wasn't about to start a silly insult tug-of-war with stupid Brad.

• Conditions at the Back to Basics Center

"What we do, for openers, is get your lives stripped down to bare essentials," Brad informed them during "chow time" number two. "You can forget about your former lifestyle, kids; all it did was get you into trouble. Up at the BBC we make things really simple for you, by means of lots of S and just the right amount of D."

"Meaning," recited Sophie, nodding while he chewed and swallowed, "that there's no TV or radio, no CDs or cassettes. No surfing on the Net, of course, no chat rooms. And no telephoning anyone at any time." Like Brad, she kept what she was eating hidden from view. When either of them took a bite, they turned and bent way over, facing forward.

"All conversation is about what's happening *right now*," said Brad, "not about the past or future." He took a swig of whatever he was drinking, a bottle that he kept inside a small brown paper bag. "We don't want to hear no bullshit 'bout the good old days or what you're gonna do when you get home again. We want you to just forget about your lousy pasts and leave your futures—starting with tomorrow—up to Soph and me."

"Trying to keep track of time is nothing but another big distraction," Sophie said. "So no student is allowed to have a watch or clock or calendar. The present, as Brad said, is all that matters. We'll always tell you what to do and when to do it. Once you're comfortable with that, we slowly let you start to make a few decisions for yourself. But that's a long way down the road. All you gotta do, for now, is just sit back, relax, and start enjoying total S and D."

Annie wasn't sure why Sophie giggled after she said that. She was finding Brad and Sophie less and less good-looking the more she heard them talk.

• The price tag on dissent

Annie didn't know if it was motion sickness or the food or the crap that she'd been hearing from her "counselors," but something made her feel a little queasy as the trip progressed. Plus, it was depressing to realize that Brad and Sophie seemed to honestly believe that it'd be good for her and Arby to become a couple of little robots, totally controlled by them. Even the principal of her old school, her parents, and her aunt and uncle weren't that extreme—although it seemed to her Judge Rowland might be.

Then Arby said out loud another thought that she'd been having: "Well, what if we don't?" he suddenly blurted out. "What if we don't do what you tell us? What if we won't do *anything*?"

"Oh, don't be stupid," Sophie told him, sounding bored. "Believe me, that's been tried; it doesn't work. And why? It's very simple. A *tribe* is like a *team*, so it requires *teamwork*. If someone doesn't work, that hurts the *team*."

Annie wondered if she was doing that deliberately, talking down to them as if they were third graders, making space between herself and them.

"Example," Sophie continued. "Let's say today I tell the Borborygmi that they're going to take a hike, and somebody decides he won't get out of bed. Well then, I'd say that *that* means *no one* takes a hike, because the Borborygmi do things as a *team*. And then I'd add: If no one takes a hike, no one gets *credit* for a hike, and *that* means no one's gotten any closer to his *graduation* day."

"So then, what's apt to happen," Brad chimed in, "is that some members of the tribe are pissed to have another member dickin' with their credits. And so, exhibiting good *teamwork*, they set about convincing lazybones to get his ass out of bed and ready for a hike—using any ways of convincing that happen to occur to them. We counselors don't have to say a word or lift a finger. We simply walk away and let the *team* supply the S and D."

"Or, to give you an example of another way it works," said Sophie, "let's say you're on a hike and you decide you aren't going to help make dinner. Simple: You don't get to eat."

"Or, like this one time when a team was digging a latrine (this is a true story, mind you)"—Brad smiled, remembering that time—"and one of them goofed off and didn't do her share of the work. Well, what the team did next was line the pit they'd dug with that kid's sleeping bag." He broke into a chuckle. "And then they held her down while they relieved themselves. Simple but effective S and D."

Arby didn't look as if he liked their answers to his questions. Annie started to suspect that at the BBC one took a lot of hikes.

• Another big concern

For the entire trip Pantagruel Primo, Esquire, just lay motionless on Annie's lap with his eyes closed. But she was sure that he was not asleep. She would have bet, also, that he was hating everything he heard every bit as much as she did—but he gave no sign of that. When, she wondered, would she have enough privacy to be able to talk with him again? To get his thinking about . . . everything? Surely, she thought, he hadn't stopped speaking to her permanently—or had he? Maybe long silences were just typical of him; she'd "had" him for some weeks before he finally spoke to (yelled at!) her the first time, during the fire.

But it was also true that she'd never hurt a little person's feelings before. Maybe with trolls and their magic-making relatives, a person got only one strike before she was out.

That thought just added to the turbulence in Annie's troubled mind, and stomach.

17.

The Borborygmi

Annie didn't think the Back to Basics Center looked at all like any school she'd ever seen or heard of, day or boarding. Nowhere on the campus was there a flat-roofed structure that resembled a factory, with lots of king-size windows through which one could see a lot of rows of one-armed, wide-armed chairs that could be moved to make a circle if the teacher had convinced herself that circles made for warmth and informality.

And neither were there any other redbrick or brownstone buildings—or even any nice, big, homey-looking two-story houses with white clapboard siding and green or black shutters and big square chimneys.

What the center really looked like was what it once had been: a summer camp for boys. So at the BBC, tribe members and their counselors lived in sixteen identical, rustic mini-chalets, grouped in two circles of eight. Between the circles were a boys' and a girls' "washhouse," each with shower rooms and sinks and toilets; the boys' room also had a long, slanted, troughlike fixture that served as a urinal. Not far from the circles of cabins was a large barnlike structure that had formerly been used as the camp's all-purpose building, where movies were shown and plays and skits put on, where arts and crafts had rooms, and where games like War and shuffleboard and other rainy-day activities took place. It now contained the center's classrooms and its auditorium. There was also a rustic dining hall, the director's bungalow (now occupied by Dr. and Mrs. Smithers), a boathouse by the small private lake, and an athletic field that had a blacktop basketball court beside it.

Each of the identical cabins contained three rooms, which nowadays were a boys' bunk room, a girls' bunk room, and between them, a common room with a fireplace and the following ten pieces of furniture: two square wooden tables and eight straight-backed chairs. In the bunk rooms there were four built-in bunks made out of two-by-sixes, with heavy canvas tacked tautly between them and thin mattresses on top of the canvas. On the end of each new student's bunk was placed a knapsack and a rolled-up sleeping bag; beside each one was a narrow wooden locker, about the size of the broom closet in Annie's old house. There was also a shelf on the wall above the head of every bed.

No kid, when seeing his or her cabin for the first time, had ever blurted out (or even thought), *Oh, wow. I know I'm going to really like it here!*

The cabins had been winterized and now were heated by

propane, in addition to their fireplaces. For light after dark, there was one kerosene lantern in each of the cabins' three rooms. The washhouses, the barn, the dining hall, and the director's bungalow all had electricity, but it was believed to be good for the kids to have them do without that particular "basic."

Annie, holding Primo still, and Arby were led to their new home-away-from-home by Sophie. The name of their cabin was painted on a piece of plywood right above its heavy door: THE FRESH START INN.

"Isn't that cute?" said Sophie, with one of her giggles. "You get a fresh start *in* The Fresh Start *Inn*." Annie tried to smile, but she couldn't do much more than grimace.

Brad joined them after a few minutes. And slouching along behind him came four other kids, two boys and two girls, the other "Borborygmi."

"Okay," said Brad when he'd gotten everyone to "grab a seat." "I'm Brad, if any of you guys missed my name before. And the lovely lady straight across from me"—he gestured toward her like an M.C. introducing the featured act—"is Sophie, your other counselor. That's all you need to know about the two of us: our names and that we're the ones who tell you what to do and when to do it for the first . . . whatever. And, I oughta add, you'll *do* those things, unless you'd like to stay here at the center for so long, your lower teeth grow through your upper lip, the way some wild boars' tusks are apt to do, sometimes."

He laughed to let them know that he was—sort of—only joking.

"But you oughta know a little more about your fellow tribesmen," he went on, "the members of your *team*, the people who you have to show us you can work with. So, for openers, suppose you go around the room and introduce yourselves. When it's your turn, what we want for you to do is tell everyone your name, including any nicknames that you'd like for us to use, along with other stuff about yourself that'll help us start to get to know you."

"For instance," Sophie followed up, "you might want to tell us what your goals are here, what kind of person you intend to be when you get out. But for heaven's sake, don't bore us with a lot of junk about how terribly misunderstood you are." She paused, then nodded at the biggest boy, an expressionless, round-headed blond with wet lips and an unhealthy pallor. "Why don't you lead off?"

The kid was over six feet tall and heavyset, and when he walked into the cabin, Annie thought he looked uncomfortable with his size, as if he hadn't learned how to handle so much bulk yet. His hips were as wide as his shoulders, and his belt made a dent between his plaid flannel shirt and his khaki trousers from the Gap. The words "big spaz" seemed made for him, thought Annie.

"You want me to say my name?" he asked Sophie, and she nodded. He seemed taken by surprise, as if that was about the last thing he expected anyone would ever ask him to do.

"Okay then, it's Kennedy—that's my first name. And Martin's my last. Or wait—*Martin* is, not Martins. I didn't mean to say *Martins*."

He smiled, not at anyone, maybe at himself; maybe he was just amused by the confusion that he thought he might have caused. He ran a hand down the top of his head, pressing his short hair straight forward, smoothing down the bangs that covered a few of the zits on his forehead. Annie got the feeling that he liked the way he looked with bangs.

"As far as having any nicknames . . . well, my mom and dad call me 'Ken' or 'Kenny,' but at school I'm mostly 'Luther,'" he went on. "Don't ask me why. This kid, Johnny Eck, he started saying 'Luther this' and 'Luther that' one day, and pretty soon, everyone was calling me that." He did that thing with his hair again and looked at Sophie, who gestured for him to go on, to say something more.

"Well, let's see," he said. "Maybe I need to learn to follow directions better. I've heard that some." He shook his head. "But what's the point of doing something stupid just 'cause someone says? I think it's stupid, having to wear stupid-looking shorts in gym, to give you one example. You know what I mean?"

When Sophie didn't agree or disagree, he said, "I used to cut myself." He made a slicing motion over the inside of one arm and then whistled a few bars of what sounded to Annie like the Happy Birthday song. "I don't know exactly why. Something to do, I guess. And not always when I was high, in case you were wondering. But I already stopped doing that a while ago, I think. I talked to this whacky shrink about it."

After taking a quick look around the room, he then dropped his eyes and stared at the space between his scuffed black Wellingtons.

"And that's my story, morning glories" was his closing line.

"All right then, Luther," Brad said, nodding. He took a quick glance at Sophie. As if concluding the job of extracting wax out of one ear, he made small circles around it with his forefinger. "I'm sure we all look forward to getting to know you better. Now, how about you, young lady?" He was looking at Annie.

Being called on second had given her time to prepare, so Annie had a little spiel all ready. She just hoped that Arby would understand what she was doing, that he wouldn't take it wrong.

"I'm Ann Ireland," she said quickly. "Everybody calls me 'Annie.' My goals are to get along with everyone and do exactly what Brad and Sophie tell me. I didn't look forward to being here, but now that I am, I plan to make the best of it. And that's really all I want to say for now. I think a person's actions speak a lot louder than their words."

She looked at all the other kids as she said that, trying to make eye contact with each of them. She wanted them to see she was a "good kid" who also planned to be a "model prisoner."

But nobody looked back except for Arby, who first puffed out his cheeks, as if about to blow lunch, but ended up by winking at her.

"O-kay," said Sophie, sounding less than totally convinced. She then looked over at the kid who'd pulled his chair away from all the others. "So, why don't you go next?" she said to him.

The kid was a sharp-featured, black-eyed little guy—Annie thought he might be a foreigner—who seemed to be the most nervous member of the tribe by far. One of his legs had the jits: Its heel kept bouncing up and down. His eyes moved jerkily about the room, like a hummingbird in a varicolored garden.

"Well," he said, "how about you people call me 'Joey'? Legally, my name is Jeremy Edward Braun, but you can forget about that. I'm going to do a name change, soon as I'm old enough. I'm going to be Maggiore Theodoracopulos, I decided. A kid at my school told me that means 'major gods love to copulate.'" He gave a nervous little laugh. "I think that's cool.

"I'm adopted, see?" he went on. "And my *real* folks are probably Greek or Italian, I bet, so my new name'll be part Italian and part Greek. But I'd rather you called me 'Joey,' kind of for short."

"All right, Joey," Sophie said. "Sounds like you're getting ready for a brand-new life. But in the short term what do you hope to accomplish here?"

"Oh, like this other girl was saying"—he jerked his head toward Annie—"I just want to get along. That shouldn't be too hard. What I figure is that all the other kids up here are fuckups, same as me. So we oughta make one happy fucked-up fami—"

"Whoa, whoa, *whoa* there!" interrupted Brad, in a hearty teacher's tone of voice. "We don't permit vulgarities up here, my little friend. Vulgarities are a real big no-no at the BBC. What they are is just a sign that someone's got a weak vocabulary. And besides, no one in our tribe's a 'fuckup.'" He looked sternly at the boy.

"The hell you say," the kid shot back at him. "You must know how to read, right? One of you must know how." He looked back and forth between Brad and Sophie. "So you've seen what's on my rap sheet, which I bet my parents sent you. You're right if you're saying I don't know about the rest of these schnozzlers. But with me, you're looking at a *major* fuckup, man."

Brad got up from his chair and in two strides was looming over the boy. He put a hand down between the base of Joey's neck and the point of his shoulder, where the trapezius muscle is, and squeezed.

"Perhaps you didn't understand me when I told you that we don't permit vulgarities up here," he said. And there was no mistaking . . . well, the threat, the *meanness* in his tone. Heartiness had been replaced by menace. "But perhaps you understand me now. *Do* you understand me, Joey?"

Annie saw the kid get red in the face. But she was pretty sure he wasn't embarrassed. She thought it was the red of rage, pure fury, although it also might have had to do with pain. His body twitched a little. His head was turned away from Brad, but she could see that his eyes were tightly closed and his lips were moving, silently giving his opinion of his present situation: *So fucked up.*

"Do you understand me, Joey?" Brad repeated, bearing down on every word and maybe squeezing even harder.

This time the kid said, "Yeah," and Brad let go and returned to his seat. Annie suspected that Joey was planning his revenge already. There was a charged silence in the room.

"So, moving right along," said Sophie cheerfully. "Suppose we hear from *this* young lady next."

The "young lady" she was looking at seemed very out of place in her present rustic surroundings, Annie thought. She had on low-rider faded jeans, a light tan, short-sleeved, tight-fitting ribbed cardigan, and (for absolutely sure) no bra. She had sandals on her feet and her toenails were painted light blue, more or less the color of her jeans. Her thick light brown hair was short and parted on one side; it kept flopping over one eye. She had a heart-shaped face, a Cupid's-bow mouth, and carefully plucked eyebrows.

She threw Sophie and the other kids a polite smile, gave a quick jerk of her head that tossed her hair back away from her face, and turned to lean toward Brad.

"Hi!" she said to him. "My *old* best friend, back home, he named me Bonnie. Like in Bonnie and Clyde? You can probably guess why, with me being sent up here and all. But my folks kept everything out of the papers and took care of people, so there weren't any charges."

She seemed to have a little trouble pronouncing some of her *r*'s, rolling them so that "friends" sounded almost like "fwiends," and "everything" close to "evewything."

"My parents didn't approve of my being Bonnie," she confided. "They pwefer boring old Emmy-Clare Street—EC, for short—like on my dwiver's license." She had a soft, husky voice that Annie thought made her sound almost too young to drive.

"But you know what? I've made a *wesolution*," she went on brightly. "To be perfect from now on. No more of that old Bonnie cwap. What I plan to do is be just like my parents want. I'm going to get real close to other people here and maybe even make myself a *new* best friend." She smiled at Brad and gave a little wiggle of excitement. Annie couldn't help but be a little jealous of her boobs—and even of her freckle-free complexion.

"Excellent." Brad beamed. He tipped back his cowboy hat and stroked his small goatee. Annie figured "cwap" was not a vulgar word in his book. "With that fine attitude, I'm betting you do everything you said. The center's here to help you be the bestest EC you can be. You play ball with us, and we'll play ball with you."

"You got yourself a deal," said ex-Bonnie, now happy to be EC again. And with that, *she* was the one who got up and walked over to Brad. But instead of seizing his trapezius, she held one open palm straight up. So he popped up himself, and they exchanged high fives.

That left Annie somewhat bug-eyed. But she peeked at Sophie and caught her looking like a mother in the park whose little boy has thrown sand out of the sandbox for the hundredth time.

Brad, however, was all wreathed in smiles.

"All *right* then," he exclaimed, then took a breath and settled down. "So, I guess it's your turn next, amigo." It was Arby time.

Annie admired Arby's strategy, which was apparent to her the moment he opened his mouth. He wanted to convince the counselors that he'd caved, that he'd abandoned any thoughts of going the rebellious route—not doing what they said. Addressing Brad and Sophie and no one else, he did everything but grovel meekly, kneel, and pull his forelock. He explained why he was known as "Arby"—making his time with the roaches sound more like a deserved punishment than a real good-paying job—and he said his purpose at the center was to make it up to his mother for the grief he'd caused her by getting himself arrested. He said he knew his life could use "a lot more positive structure."

It seemed to Annie that their far-from-genius-level keepers swallowed his act hook, line, and sinker—that they were probably congratulating themselves on one hugely successful intimidation job back there in the van. They nodded approvingly as he spoke, sure that this was one kid who would sprint right off and dig latrines when he was told to.

"Fair enough," said Sophie when he'd finished. "You've got

the right idea, my boy. Which leaves the sixth and final member of our tribe. And you are . . . ?"

"Jennifer Redmond," snapped the girl who she was looking at, "though the kids back home call me 'Ragweed,' or just 'Weed,' for short. A lot of people seem to be allergic to the way I am. I can't imagine why."

Annie almost smiled. It didn't take a high IQ to know that this Ragweed kid was doing almost anything she could to produce allergic reactions—at least in people over thirty, most Republicans, and any member of a labor union or a choir. She'd dyed her short straight hair that reddish-purplish color many newly minted punks try out; she had a tongue stud and three eyebrow rings. Her outfit was all black and almost a total cliché: black jeans (with a heavy silver chain hanging from one belt loop and disappearing into a pocket), black Doc Martens, and a black boat-necked top under the one not-totally-clichéd item, a black tuxedo jacket (cuffs rolled back) with shiny velvet lapels. If she'd been the type to shop at Wal-Mart, she'd have had to make her selections from the plus-size racks.

The more Annie looked at her, though, the more she realized that, with a complete makeover and maybe a few less pounds, this Ragweed would be pretty cute. Not Fleur-glamorous (lacking those long legs), but definitely nice-looking. But then she realized *that* was a cliché, her thinking that.

"Didn't your mothuh teach you that it's rude to stare?" Ragweed's sudden question snapped Annie out of her reverie.

"I hate to tell you this, but somebody your age who's still play-ing with dolls has forfeited her right to stare at *any*body." And then she stared at Pantagruel Primo with unmistakable disgust, making a point of doing so, thought Annie.

"I wondered about the doll myself, no kidding," EC said in an aside to Brad. "I know she's in the tribe and all, but is this Annie person maybe just a bit retarded?"

Annie felt her ears get warm. "It's for a school project," she told them. "The judge said I should bring it here." That wasn't a total lie. "If you don't like it, too bad." She was mad at herself for calling Primo "it" instead of "him."

"Oh, sure—right," said Ragweed. "I bet a judge *would* order something like that. And me, I dress this way 'cause I'm in mourning for my daddy, who was archduke of Bohemia."

"Hey!" said Sophie. "Cut that out, all three of you. No bick-ering in this tribe. I shouldn't have to remind you that none of you is perfect now, or ever will be." (*Was that put-down arrowed at EC?* Annie wondered.) "We don't call anybody names here; everybody gets along with everyone or else."

Ragweed heaved a big sigh and looked away from her. It was the kind of sigh familiar to most women who share homes with teenage girls. The kind of sigh that says, *Of all the mothers in the world, why is mine the stupidest?*

Annie, though, believed she saw an opportunity for scoring brownie points while simultaneously shining up her "good-kid" image. So she stuck a hand out at this Ragweed character and said, "If I was staring, I'm sorry. I absolutely didn't mean to." She let out a little laugh. "I don't feel at all allergic to you." Then she tossed a smile at EC. "Or to you, either."

Ragweed's eyes narrowed when she saw Annie's extended hand. Annie had the feeling that the other girl had seen right through her ploy—and maybe also thought it was a good one. Slowly, slowly, she put out her own hand and dropped it into Annie's. But she didn't squeeze. It lay there like a trout left on a riverbank out in the summer sun.

"That's *wonderful*," gushed Ragweed, with obviously phony sincerity. "And I wish *all* the best to you and yours." That last was said with another look at Primo, a look Annie thought to be more mischievous than mean this time. "After all, we both are Borborygmi, fellow members of the best darn tribe in the entire BBC."

Annie couldn't help herself: She grinned at Ragweed. The other girl *had* seen what she had tried to do and then had done her one better. In Annie's grin was pure and honest admiration.

Ragweed then grinned back at her and gave her just about the fastest wink that Annie'd ever seen. EC looked confused by what was going on.

"Well, that's better, both of you," said Sophie, completely missing what had happened. "And now I think it's time to meet with Dr. Smithers."

18.

Brief Encounters of All Kinds

Dr. Smithers had an office in the barn, and it was to that office Brad and Sophie brought the Borborygmi.

It was a peculiar sort of office, Annie thought, in that anyone who walked into the barn could see right into it. Of course, this also meant that Smithers could see out of it.

In actual fact, his desk was located near the far end of the barn's wide hallway—the one that had the center's classrooms on either side of it. To insulate the good doctor from the noise in the hall, and also to keep his conversations private, there were full-length glass windows and a glass door across the width of the hallway, but they did nothing to lessen the impression that the director was very much involved in the daily life of the school. (Or, as the students liked to say, "Pig Smithers is watching you.") Right behind his desk there was an enormous picture window that made it possible for him, if he just swiveled around, to check on what was happening outside.

Walking down the hall toward the director's office, Annie

glanced into a couple of classrooms and made some interesting discoveries. One was that all the kids she saw were dressed the same, in olive drab; their boots and pants and jackets looked a good deal like army fatigues, the clothes that soldiers wear while doing nonmilitary cleanup jobs. The other was that, in terms of posture and attitude, they resembled kids in classes back home. A lot of them looked sort of stunned, less like participants than people having something done to them, something that they either didn't care about or (possibly) resented.

She could also see there wasn't anyone in the glass-fronted room at the end of the corridor.

That didn't seem to bother Brad and Sophie; they didn't pause a heartbeat on the threshold of the office. Sophie reached right out and grabbed the doorknob, turned it, and pushed. Moments later, the six kids were seated on six straight-backed chairs facing the doctor's desk, while Brad and Sophie settled on the comfy little couch off to one side.

The Borborygmi didn't have to wait too long.

"Ah, yes . . . sorry . . . don't get up," Annie and the others heard—in a soft, apologetic tone of voice—as the door behind them opened to admit two people, the first of them William McGuffey Smithers, director of the Back to Basics Center.

Dr. Smithers's "look" was very different from Brad's and Sophie's, as well as from that of the kids whom Annie'd seen. Unlike students and staff, he wasn't really dressed for outdoor activities, other than perhaps short walks from house or hunting lodge to car, or vice versa. But he was definitely a tweedbag, with his little wool cap and almost matching wool sports coat, one with leather patches on its elbows and on the front of one shoulder. Under the jacket was an oxford cloth shirt, light blue, and a striped silk tie, and below the waist he had on creased gray flannel trousers and shiny wing-tip shoes, dark brown.

With him came a tall woman with a face resembling a llama's, Annie thought: big on lips and weariness, foreign to the situation she was in. She had on a long, full skirt, mostly green and yellow with a little brilliant red, a skirt that celebrated palm fronds and exotic fruits. She also wore a white silk shirt, wrapped in a fringed black shawl. Her hair was cut quite short and piled high in ringlets in the front.

She went directly to a chair off to one side, sat down, and from the Little Orphan Annie lunch box she was carrying, extracted cigarettes and matches, headphones, and a CD player. Dr. Smithers paid her no attention, didn't even seem to notice she was there.

"So, now . . . yes . . . very good," he said, settling into the leather chair behind his desk while taking off his cap. He wiggled his butt a couple of times to get more comfortable. "And you would be . . ."—he put his elbows on the desk and fitted the fingertips of his left hand to the widespread fingertips of his right—". . . the Borborygmi!"

Somewhat to Annie's surprise, Smithers was as bald as the Daddy Warbucks painting on the woman's lunch box; his dome was smooth and shiny, even on the sides and back. But that didn't mean he couldn't grow good hair crops elsewhere. He had eyebrows that were like big shaggy caterpillars and a salt-and-pepper beard and mustache combo, trimmed short and tightly wrapped around his face like indoor-outdoor carpeting. But he didn't look the least bit fierce or "Wanted." The eyes under those heavy brows were a surprising light blue, and like the boy Joey's, they never settled very long on anything or anyone. But where Joey mostly seemed pissed off and alienated, Smithers looked uneasy, even weary.

"On behalf of the entire staff," he started, finally, as if he'd found his place somewhere in the folder of his memory, "and, yes, the student body of the Back to Basics Center . . . I do welcome you to . . . well"—his eyes went to the ceiling, as if searching for a word up there—". . . our *midst*. I trust that . . ."—he looked over at the couch, maybe checking on its contents—"Brad and . . . and, uh, his capable *associate* have begun to introduce you to our program here."

At that point his mouth widened and the kids could see his upper teeth beneath that mighty mustache. Annie thought he looked like the actor in the Tums TV commercial, before he got relief, but she was pretty sure the doctor thought that he was smiling.

"Many of our students are at first . . . *discomforted*," he went on, "by our—the Back to Basics Center's—*basicness*. They may also be surprised to learn what sacrifices their moms . . . or dads . . . or court-appointed guardians agree to endure when they enroll them here. Results like ours cost money." He licked his lips.

"A lot of money. Two hundred and fifty dollars every day you're here. That's seventeen fifty a week and more than seven thousand dollars a month." He rattled off those numbers with no hesitation whatsoever.

"They are willing to forgo," he said, one finger raised as if to make a special call for their attention, "a trip abroad or perhaps a brand-new Volvo wagon in order to receive—delivered unto them—a new, improved, rebuilt son or daughter."

Just as he said that, a boy appeared in the window right behind him, a student at the center, Annie guessed, going by his age and olive drab outfit. He stood motionless at first, as if sizing up the scene in front of him: six strange kids about his age, not yet in uniform, being addressed by the director. Then he raised both arms and started swinging them back and forth over his head, like a person on a curvy mountain road signaling a car to stop before it crashed into the mud slide just ahead. And as he did so he also shook his head and mouthed, repeatedly, the one word *No, no, no, no, no*. After that he mimed the placing of a noose around his neck and tightening the rope until his tongue came out and his head flopped over, dead. Then, quick as he'd appeared, he hurried off.

"And rebuilt by the program all of you will be," continued Dr. Smithers, unaware that a negative endorsement of that program had just been acted out behind him. "You'll be changed in terms of your priorities, your habits, and your d-d-d . . ." He blinked rapidly, three or four times, then looked over (beseechingly, thought Annie) at the twosome on the couch.

"Decision making," Brad provided.

"Yes, quite right. Your decision making, D. Your 'PHD': priorities, habits, and decision making," said Smithers, nodding. "And once you see—"

He was interrupted by the woman in the chair off to one side. She'd been sitting calmly, smoking, looking down, with headphones on, but recently, one Birkenstocked foot had started tapping. And then suddenly she burst enthusiastically into song, not too melodically, but loudly. *"Saturday night's all right!"* she sang—or "chanted," one could say.

Annie looked at Arby, who raised his eyebrows and grinned.

"Elton John!" EC cried out, and clapped her hands together.

Dr. Smithers didn't share her pleasure. He shouted at the woman, "Hey, Dolores!" And when she looked up at him, "Cut out the caterwauling, damn it!"

The woman pantomimed contrition with a naughty little smile and the touching of her mouth with fingertips.

"Oops. Sorry, dear," she said.

"So *that*, said John, is that," said Dr. Smithers, forgetting he'd been in the middle of a sentence and now ignoring the woman again. He got to his feet. Annie got the feeling he was on autopilot, saying lines he'd memorized long since.

"I'll give your folks a call," the doctor said, "and tell them that we've had this pleasant little chat and that you're fitting in just fine already. I'll also tell them I've assured you that whenever you're on campus, you should feel completely free to visit with me here at any time. My door is always open, Sundays and holidays included. Whether I'm here or not." And he gave a little laugh.

"Borborygmi!" he concluded. "Go with God—and blessings on you all."

His blessing seemed to be a signal Brad and Sophie understood. They rose together and, in the absence of God, said, "Let's move it," as they led their little tribe away.

The rest of the day included a stop at the "commissary," where the kids were issued a set of "school clothes" for which their parents (or whoever) would be charged sums something like what they'd have paid for outfits at, say, Prada or Chanel. They were also involved with a couple of heavy-on-the-whole-grains meals at the dining hall and with various preparations for their first hike, which was to begin the very next day and would continue (in Sophie's unspecific words) "awhile."

Before they went to bed that night, EC took a look at Primo, who was lying propped on Annie's pillow, pointed at the guy, and said to no one in particular, "That thing is freaking me out, you know. It makes me think I'm living with a feeb who never heard of birth control or something."

"Well, just don't look at him," said Good Citizen Annie mildly, knowing Sophie was monitoring their conversation. "I'm very much pro-birth control, believe me. And like I said, I'm only following the judge's orders. Though, to tell you the truth, I've gotten to kind of like my little friend."

She hoped P. Primo would recognize the truthfulness of that.

Once she was in bed, with Primo safely there beside her, it took Annie quite a while to fall asleep.

She thought about what Sophie'd said, back there in the van, about her parents not having "fed her the right stuff," meaning structure and discipline, apparently. But Sophie'd been wrong about that. The life they'd made her lead was full of structure. And discipline? Heck, she'd been made to do things all her life. Not only that, she'd been a willing victim: She'd played along, obeyed, tried hard to please her parents, not to mention her teachers, coaches, people whom she'd baby-sat for, and so on. Compared to a whole lot of kids she could name, she hadn't behaved "badly" (as Sophie seemed to think she had) at all.

What her life at home had lacked, she now thought, was not S and D, but C—conversations, real conversations. Her parents talked *to* her, all right. They *told* her stuff: what they expected, what she ought to do, what she should be doing next. Sometimes, they'd throw a question in there, like "How was school?" or they'd ask her to tell them about her day. But they would have had a cow if she had told them any of the truly interesting things that happened at school, if she had said, *Well, Amos Drumby told me he could score some Ecstasy.* No conversation would have followed that announcement. Oh, her parents would have screamed and yelled and carried on about kids and drugs and "The Law," and about how they certainly hoped she'd avoid Amos Drumby and his rotten ilk. They might even have said they'd been around a lot of drugs when they were growing up and so they knew only too well, from firsthand experience, what "scoring Ecstasy" could lead to. And that would have been the end of it. It was as if they didn't care to know what *she* thought about Amos Drumby and Ecstasy. Her parents acted as if, in the Ireland family, *they* had all the power (which was sort of true) and also all the knowledge, insights, and worthwhile opinions (which didn't seem true at all).

Annie could feel Pantagruel Primo's hard little body up against her shoulder as she thought those thoughts. And it suddenly crossed her mind that, in one respect, she was sort of like his parent! She had all the power, or at least all of a certain kind of power, and she'd used it, or the threat of it, *disgustingly*, that very day. She'd threatened him in much the same way her parents had threatened her a couple of times: "Well, how'd you like it if . . . ?" she'd said.

My God, she thought. *I'm going to* be *my parents if I don't watch out.*

That thought depressed her even more than being in the Fresh Start Inn did, at least for that moment. It was easy for her to say (as she had to Arby more than once), "When *I* grow up, I'll *never* do such and such," some thing that *they* did. But wouldn't she? Was there maybe just this one way of behaving that more or less took you over when you got to be a certain age and had kids of your own—the way that you remembered from your childhood? Maybe all your good intentions would be blown away as soon as you felt stressed, or defied, or had a headache, or otherwise felt sorry for yourself.

Without further thought, she ducked her head under the covers, then pulled the doll down too and got her lips against its ear.

"Primo," she whispered, "Mister Primo, I am so, so sorry for the way I acted in the van. *I* got us into this, if either of us did, not you at all. So I've no right to think you ought to get us out of here. I understand you've got a ton of rules you have to follow, same as I do. All I want is for the three of us—you, me, and Arby—to stay friends whatever happens. If we stick together, I just know we'll manage to get safely out of here, somehow."

And Primo *answered*! She could barely catch his whisper back, but because she'd heard him say the words before, she recognized them right away.

"Felicitously phrased," he said.

19.

Ready, Hike!

The morning of the next day was for preparations—everybody getting ready for the hike. In practical terms, that meant the kids bringing all the "supplies" that they'd be packing to the common room of the Fresh Start Inn and then dividing these up among their six big backpacks. Meanwhile, Brad and Sophie went off to the director's house to pick up the things that *they* would carry, tell the doctor where they planned to go, and pick up the map that ought to help them to get there and back.

"I volunteer to be the tribal chef," said Ragweed, eyeballing the heap of plastic bags on one of the square wooden tables: freeze-dried meals, dehydrated this and that (including sauces), as well as rice and beans and pasta. She picked up one of the bags and then another, checking out their labels.

"My secret for turning all this crap into delicious hearty dining?" she continued. "Oh, all right, you've wormed it out of me. It's 'Just add water.' See? Those magic words appear on every package. All you peons have to do is find fresh water and lug it to my campfire, which I'll have made by rubbing Brad and Sophie together. It may take a lot of trips, a lot of lugging, but I have faith in you. Then I will do the really hard part: adding water to whatever's in my cooking pot."

"'Taco sauce,'" Luther read off one of the envelopes. "I vote we get to have a lot of tacos. Mexican food's my favorite. Anytime we have Mexican and you don't like it, you can give me yours—'specially if it's real hot." He smacked his lips, anticipating supersize portions of his favorite spicy stuff.

Annie couldn't get over how different almost everyone looked in their center uniforms. Luther was the exception, perhaps because he was the biggest and so didn't seem to be engulfed by shapeless olive drab. EC despised the stiff material that paid no heed to the contours of her body. In an attempt to give her look a little style, she'd tied one of her khaki handkerchiefs around her neck, but all that did was make her look as if her throat was sore or she was trying to hide a hickey. Annie hadn't noticed if she'd put on one of her issued bras; now you couldn't tell, given how her shirt and jacket hung on her.

Joey looked the most like a convict in his uniform, Annie thought: the weasely little guy in a prison flick who snipes at guards and stooges for the tattooed giant all the other cons steer clear of. Ragweed had rolled her sleeves and pant legs halfway up her shins and forearms, making sure she didn't look the same as everybody else.

Annie thought she and Arby looked like kids she'd once seen pictures of in *USA Weekend*, kids in a Romanian orphanage.

In addition to the food and extra socks and underwear, the kids packed pots and pans and sleeping bags, foam pads, some lengths of nylon rope and tarpaulins—those last to use for making shelters in the wild.

Annie also had to save some space for Primo.

"Hey, give me a break," EC complained when she saw the doll's head sticking out of Annie's pack. "You're taking *that* along? Why don't you leave the dumb thing here? I promise not to tell the judge on you. It isn't fair that I have to take a big old heavy frying pan so you can have room for your stupid *toy!*"

"Brad and Sophie said I should take him," Annie improvised, bending the truth, but not a whole lot. "So that's what I'm doing. You don't like it? Tough." Her freckles stood out against the strained whiteness of her face. In Brad and Sophie's absence she didn't feel the need to be Miss Perfect Tribesperson. To her relief, none of the other three strangers seemed to care about Primo one way or the other.

"You know what's kinda strange?" said Joey. "What isn't here at all." He gestured at their packs. "We don't have no tools for cuttin' firewood, like saws or axes. And how we meant to dig a hole to crap in if we haven't got some kind of shovel or a spade? Also, I saw we got a bunch of different-size forks and spoons but not a single knife. What if we catch a fish and want to clean it?"

"Don't you worry," Ragweed told him. "I bet Brad and Sophie'll have everything we need and then some. But we'll get to use it only if we have permission. They wouldn't trust a fuckup with a big old axe, I don't believe," she said to Joey, grinning at the guy, maybe baiting him a little, Annie thought. They were all sitting on those straight-backed chairs by then, the six of them around one table.

"And maybe they'll bring along a little thing of poison, too," she went on, making her voice sound sinister, "and they'll slip it into our Kool-Aid once we've gotten to a good place for them to dispose of our bodies. I read this novel in school last year about some kids whose parents sent them to this boarding school where the deal was that the kids would be, like, gotten rid of." She laughed. "I loved that book. In the end the kids won out, of course."

"Jeezum!" Joey said, eyes widening. "That could be the deal with us! I'm adopted, right? So what I'm like is an appliance that my parents got at Sears or Wal-Mart, and took home, and found out it didn't work right. But seeing as they'd used it, the store wouldn't take it back, so they hadda pay someone to come get it and dispose of it some way. I bet that Brad would *love* to off a bunch of kids. You see the way he grabbed me yesterday? The guy's a *killer*."

"You think?" said Luther. He pursed his lips and wrinkled up his brow. "Nowadays, they say it's possible to order any-thing—like off the Internet? I heard my mother say that. So getting someone to kill a kid probably isn't all that hard, if you know where to look. I could see *my* parents going for a deal like that." He shrugged and nodded.

"Hey, wait. Time out," said Ragweed, making a *T* with two

stiff hands. "I was only *kidding*, man. They're not going to kill us here. Long as we're alive, our folks are paying this place a shitload of money. You heard what Smithers said—how much that is. No one's going to kill a cash cow. This is America, man."

"Oh, I don't know," EC chimed in. "What Smithers said was what they had to pay while we were here. But suppose he had a different rate for killing kids, a much, much higher one. Twenty thousand apiece, let's say. So if they did all six of us, that'd be, like . . ."—she paused, then counted, going around the table, starting with herself—". . . twenty, forty, sixty, eighty, a hundred, a hundred and twenty thousand, all in one fell swoop. And then they'd have room for six more kids who they could kill. I can tell you this much—and I'm not shittin' you—my mother (she's my stepmom, really), she would dearly love to see the last of *me*."

Annie could almost believe that. EC, it seemed to her, was stupid, shallow, conceited, and obnoxious, for sure. But still, she didn't think it was remotely possible that *her* parents would pay anyone to kill her. They just weren't that kind of people. And she was double sure about Arby's mom and uncle; they absolutely *doted* on the kid. But while she was still deciding whether or not to say anything herself—and if so, what—Joey spoke up again.

"Look," he said. "Let's say we can't be a hundred percent sure about what this Brad and Sophie are going to do, one way or the other. But if we just sit back and don't do nothing, and they *are* planning to kill us, we wouldn't know it until it happened, and we're dead. So how about this? There's six of us and only two of them. Three against one's good odds in any kind of fight. If we plan it right, I bet you we could *overpower* them and make a break. Bust outta here—*escape*! And we oughta do that pretty quick, you know? Real early in this hike we're going on. Before they can do anything to *us*!"

"What? Now you're talking about us killing *Brad* and *Sophie*?" Arby said suddenly. "That's completely crazy! We'd get caught in no time flat and thrown in jail. I've *been* in jail—and so has Annie—and believe me, jail makes this place look like . . . I don't know, a plush *resort* or something. I'm not agreeing to murder anyone, or to be an accessory, either. I'd run and tell Smithers first."

"Who said anything about murder?" Joey asked. "I said *overpower* them, dickhead—and then, like maybe tie 'em to a tree and leave 'em. And once we've got away, we could call up old man Smithers and tell him where they are. They'd miss a meal or two or three is all. If we had a gun, some kind of weapon like that, we wouldn't hardly have to *touch* them."

Annie thought that he was just BS-ing. They didn't have a gun. Brad and Sophie were (a) bigger and in shape and strong and (b) would be the only ones who had anything that could be used as a weapon. Joey was mad at Brad and would have loved to get back at him, but he was just flapping his gums when he talked about "overpowering" the two counselors. That wasn't going to—couldn't—happen. She was pretty sure the other kids would see how basically powerless they were. But then . . .

"I've got a blade, if that'd help," said Luther. "Look. I had it in my boot before. I could hold it up against old Sophie's Adam's apple. . . ."

He'd reached under the back of his jacket and, from the waistband of his pants, pulled out what could have been—but wasn't—a flattened, double-wide fountain pen. He pressed a button on its side and . . . *schwip*! Quick as light, a five-inch blade leaped out, all sharp and shiny.

"All right!" cried Joey, black eyes gleaming.

Oops, thought Annie.

"This is *exciting*," EC told the room. Before, she'd been all over Brad, but just like that, she'd made the switch to anti-Brad, no sweat.

What Annie desperately wanted to hear at that point was something from Ragweed. If Ragweed would only hurry up and dump on Joey's wild idea, then it'd be three against three, and after a while maybe Luther or even EC would see that it'd be a big mistake to pull a knife on Brad or Sophie—and that it was just being paranoid to believe their parents were paying to have them killed. Ragweed was a nonconformist, but she wasn't dumb. Ragweed might inject a little common sense into this conversation, Annie thought.

Almost in answer to her thought, Ragweed started talking. "Hmm," she said first. She shook her head and squinched up her nose and turned her eyes into slits, as if she was about to sneeze.

"I don't know. As a committed pacifist, I'm totally antiviolence. But I could go along with, like, *restraining* someone, I guess."

She said all that in a low voice, more to herself than to the group, while looking at the tabletop. But then she took a deep breath, picked up her head, and spoke to everyone, in a clear and certain tone of voice. "Okay. Here's what I think," she said. "I don't believe they're actually planning to kill us. But I sure do hate this place and the whole idea of going on a lot of stupid hikes. The less time I spend here the better. So escaping sounds pretty good to me, and I'll help to make that happen, on two conditions. One, that everybody swears they won't engage in any violence—no using Luther's knife except to threaten someone, right? And second, that all six of us are in on this, that everyone agrees it's a good idea."

She looked first at Annie and then at Arby as she spoke that second condition.

Annie's first reaction to it was: *We're screwed.* If they didn't go along with this idea (which wasn't even close to being a *plan* yet) they'd be rats, outsiders, even enemies (of people they'd be living with for God knows how long). But if they agreed to be a part of an attempted escape that failed (as this one probably would), chances were they'd have (be given) an even worse time at the center than they were in for now.

She looked at Arby. He looked back at her. She couldn't tell from his expression what he was thinking. She figured her face looked the same. They had to speak, say something. Everybody was looking at them now.

But before she started, she glanced across the room at Primo. His head was still sticking out of her backpack; he looked wide awake and thoughtful, involved. She needed his opinion. For any plan of theirs to work, his approval was essential; scheming was a specialty of his. If he chose to use his powers, he could doom—or help to make successful—anything the group came up with.

He didn't keep her waiting. His head went up and down, almost imperceptibly. She let out the breath she hadn't realized she'd been holding.

"I can't say this is a *great* idea," she said, "but it may be good enough. So I'm not opposed to giving it a try. I never wanted to come here, which means, of course, I'd love to leave. As long as we're agreed—like Ragweed said—that no one's going to get hurt, I'll be in on whatever plan we come up with."

She looked at Arby as she finished saying that and saw his eyes come back from where he'd had them aimed: across the room, at Primo.

"I feel the same as her, I guess," said Arby.

Annie smiled and nodded—apprehensive still, not optimistic, but at least a little hopeful.

The three of them were going into this together, come what may.

20

The First Day Out

Arby's cousin Ernie Stiletto had endured—and proudly survived—Marine Corps Basic Training down at Parris Island, so of course Arby had heard a great deal about the hikes (under full packs) that were a painful part of it. But he was almost certainly exaggerating when he told Annie, near the end of their first day of hiking, that she was being made to do everything that was required of a Marine recruit "and then some."

Even allowing for exaggeration, though, the Borborygmi did put in a long, hard day. Brad and Sophie never had been master sergeants or drill instructors, but they did have much in common with those military taskmasters. Using a combination of encouragement and threats, congratulations and abuse, they kept their charges moving for most of an entire morning and a good chunk of the afternoon. They did stop once beside a stream for a lunch of PowerBars and trail mix, washed down with clear, cold water, and they also called brief halts to "answer nature's yoo-hoos and get your little batteries recharged," but the rest of the day they walked—on logging roads and deer trails, up hills and down their other sides, on and on and on. To nowhere in particular, it seemed.

Annie learned two facts about Brad and Sophie in the course of the day—three, if you count her full awareness that they'd done this same routine before. The first was: Like most good coaches, they were skillful psychologists; they knew how to get the most out of their charges. At times, they told the Borborygmi that they were, beyond a shadow of a doubt, the best tribe ever to have graced the center—that they were going farther and faster on this, their very first day, than groups made up of older kids, all of whom had been outstanding high school athletes, all-staters all, in fact. At other times, they chided individuals by name, accusing them of slowing down the group and showing "zip self-discipline." They reminded one and all that they were being graded (on a scale of "one-oh-oh") on their "hikeability and attitude" and that these grades would have a bearing on their graduation dates. "Pissers and moaners," they said, lowered the group grade that the whole tribe got collectively.

The second fact she learned was pretty much a confirmation of something she'd suspected all along: Brad and Sophie were, themselves, in world-class shape. Going up the steepest hills, they didn't even breathe hard; judging by the easy way they handled them, you would have thought their bulky packs were filled with balsa wood (instead of gourmet meals, spare Gore-Tex hiking boots from L.L. Bean, some sharp and heavy tools, and other extras). During those three rest stops, when the kids flopped down and some took off their boots to give their poor sore feet a rub, Brad and Sophie just stayed standing, looking at their "topo" map and taking compass readings. When someone asked her "how much farther?" Sophie grinned and then tossed off a little mangled Robert Frost: "There's miles to go before *you* sleep," she said.

In Annie's estimation, it was going to be no easy matter to "overpower" this pair—assuming Joey and the others even had the energy to try, after many, many hours on the trail. When they finally stopped and before they began to make camp at the end of that first day, she could tell by looking at her fellow tribe members that "overpowering" couldn't possibly occur until tomorrow or the next day, until they'd gotten more used to this exhausting "basic."

"Don't get too relaxed," Brad told the kids when they'd finally reached the clearing in the woods he called "Camp One." They were all sitting on the ground or on the trunk of a fallen tree. "The first thing we do when we arrive at camp is get it all set up. For a few days that'll take a while, because you won't know what you're doing. The thing is—see?—that me 'n' Sophie aren't going to help you much. You're probably gonna mess up pretty bad for a while. But this way, when you've figured something out for yourselves, you'll really have it learned. So now, and first of all, we'll do a little unpacking and then divvy up the chores."

Groaning, the kids struggled to their feet again, wanting to get "the chores" over with so they could finally—*finally*—kick back and relax. To begin with, everyone extracted from their packs all the things that had to do with cooking, and eating, and sleeping, and making shelters. Annie had to take Pantagruel Primo out of her knapsack so she could get at the food packets she had in there.

Brad and Sophie then assigned the kids their jobs. Joey and Ragweed were told to use the tarps and ropes to make two shelters, each one big enough to house four people, males in one, females in the other. Luther got the hauling wood detail; he was meant to roam around and find dry firewood and bring it to Brad and Sophie, who would chop and saw it into proper lengths.

Brad handed EC a little fire-starting kit and told her she should first collect big stones, put them in a circle, and then make their campfire in it.

"There aren't any matches here," she pointed out once she'd opened up the kit and seen the various items it contained.

"That's right," Sophie agreed. "Just follow the directions, sweetie."

"It really isn't all that hard," a cheerful Brad assured her.

"And finally," he said, "for our remaining pair of eager beavers, another job that everyone will thank them for, assuming nobody falls in. The digging of our . . . comfort stations. Using this."

From behind his back he produced a little spade. It was bigger than the one that Annie'd had for digging in her sandbox, years before, but not a whole lot bigger. He handed it to Arby.

"Dig two," he told them. "One this-a-way and one that-a-way"—he pointed first to his left and then to his right—"so boys and girls can do their business separately. And make them far enough away from here so we won't even know they're there, no matter where the wind is coming from. And make them big enough so we can use them . . . comfortably."

Annie suspected they'd been given the hardest job on purpose, sort of as a test. Did they really plan (as they had said) "to make the best of things?" She was determined not to flunk the test. Scowl free, she got up and followed Arby as he headed "this-a-way." She scooped up Primo without even breaking stride.

When they'd gone far enough to be out of earshot, Arby stopped and jammed the spade into the ground.

"Look at that pathetic little thing," he said to Annie. "It'll take forever to dig a decent hole with it. And what'd he mean by 'comfortably'? How big's it going to have to be?"

As if energized by Arby's put-down, the little spade began to move. All on its own—as a pair of teenage jaws flopped open—it scooped up some dirt and put it to one side. Then it went back for more and did the same, again and again, moving rapidly, assertively, getting into a good rhythm.

Annie just assumed she was hallucinating, that she was a victim of exhaustion. She sat down before she fell down. She wondered if she was just about to faint or maybe die.

But then she heard the voice of Primo, solemnly reciting:

"In a hole in the ground there lived a hobbit. Not a nasty, dirty wet hole, filled with the ends of worms and an oozy smell, nor yet a dry, bare, sandy hole with nothing in it to sit down on or to eat; it was a hobbit hole and that means *comfort*."

Arby, who was still standing, had turned to look at the little fellow. "You're quoting J. R. R. Tolkien's *The Hobbit*," he said.

"Good boy. Exactly right," said Primo, and Annie saw that he was smiling. "And though it won't be a hobbit hole your spade is digging—I've seen a lot of *them*, of course—it should be one your people *can* use, just as Brad requested, 'comfortably.' Why don't you just sit down and watch the ever pleasant spectacle of a hard job being done by someone—something—else?"

Arby was pleased to do exactly that. He and Annie sat there—she with Primo on her lap—and watched the skillful spade dig out as neat and sizable a hole as any group of campers would require. The dirt it had removed was piled beside the hole so that departing . . . customers could shove some in before they left and, finally, leave the site appearing just as pure and natural as it had been before a bunch of human beings came that way.

Then, Annie, Arby, Primo, and the spade went "that-a-way," around to the other side of the campsite, where the energetic spade proceeded to dig another hole, every bit as perfect as the first one.

When they all returned to the campsite, they saw that

the other tribespeople had had—were having—quite a lot of trouble with *their* chores. The "shelters" that Joey and Ragweed were constructing sagged ominously and didn't look as if they'd provide much shelter if a strong wind came along, let alone a thunderstorm. A little ways away, Brad and Sophie were explaining to Luther, in exasperated tones, that a length of rotten birch could *not* be used as firewood.

EC, in the center of the campsite, was staring at her fire-starting kit while informing one and all that the damn thing didn't work. "I bet you *nobody* could start a fire with *this*," she said, throwing the kit's components on the ground and stomping off in Brad's direction.

"Oh, I betcha *someone* can," said Primo quietly, with a nod in the fireplace's direction. "Let's give it a try."

They went and hunkered down beside the ring of stones. Following Primo's instructions, Annie and Arby made a little pyramid of the twigs and leaves EC had collected, and then they lined up the contents of the kit.

"Now," said Primo, looking down at the kit stuff. And then, to their amazement, the little guy began to sing, just very softly. "'*Come on, baby, light my fire . . .*'" were the lines he sang, sounding really quite a lot like Jim Morrison of the Doors.

At once, the items from the kit were activated. Bits of wood and then of metal (magnesium, it turned out to be) were shaved and added to the pyramid of twigs and leaves. Then the provided flint and steel collided, sending streams of sparks onto the flammable materials, which (just as they were meant to do) first smoldered before bursting into flames. On this tiny fire Annie and Arby added bigger and bigger sticks (as Primo told them to) until they had a good thing going.

When she heard the fire's crackling—or maybe smelled its smoke—EC (who'd been whining at the unresponsive backs of Brad and Sophie) spun around and yelled, "How'd you do that, anyway? You had *matches*, right?"

Annie and Arby shook their heads but didn't answer. Primo smirked, but he was turned away from her, so EC couldn't see his face.

"They think they're so *hot*," she said to Brad and Sophie. "But I bet you they had matches. I hope you're going to search them."

Brad and Sophie didn't search them. But after supper (macaroni and cheese à la Ragweed for the kids, beef bourguignonne prepared by Sophie for herself and Brad) they did comment favorably on both the fire and the "comfort stations," saying that it looked as if they might have a couple of "young Kit Carsons" in their midst.

"And mentioning Kit Carson," Sophie said, "reminds me that I should mention local wildlife—the animals Kit might have shot if he'd been guiding in this neighborhood. For openers, there's two old favorites, deer and bear—black bears, no grizzlies—and also cougars and coyotes, possibly a wolf or two. All of them are kind of shy, though if they're hungry enough and get a whiff of what we're eating, they could come to see if they could swipe a bite or two. That's why, each night, we're going to put our food supply in a couple of knapsacks and hang them from a branch." She looked around and pointed. "Tonight, right over there. High enough so no wild thing can reach them."

"Some other little moochers might not be so shy," Brad added. "Raccoons and skunks and porcupines are all pretty curious—raccoons, especially. If you hear some rustling at night, it might be one of them. Oh, and if you ever see one in the daytime and it doesn't run away, look out. It'll probably have rabies." He chuckled. "And you wouldn't want to catch yourself a dose of *that*, believe me."

That night Annie made sure to put her sleeping bag up against the canvas wall at the back of the ladies' shelter, figuring that if a hungry wolf or cougar sauntered in the front and started eating people, it'd be full long before it got to her and Primo. She was glad when Ragweed came and crawled into her sleeping bag beside her and when Sophie lay down next to *her*. That meant EC, who now seemed to have it in for her as well as Primo, would not only have a hard time doing anything to either of them while they were sleeping, but also would play the part of appetizer, if there was to be a cougar's blue plate dinner special.

Having had that soothing thought, Annie closed her eyes and slept nine solid hours.

21.

Sam T. Quincy, District Forester

Before they got the kids busy breaking camp the next morning, Brad and Sophie consulted their map and warned the tribe the hike to "Camp Two" was going to be a "longie."

"You know how it is in that big bike race?" Sophie said. "The Tour duh France? Some days it's so-and-so-many miles with a lot of ups and downs, and other days it's maybe twice that many miles but mostly flat. Well, today's leg of *this* little tour has got a lot of ups and downs in it, but it's also pretty long. So get ready for a toughish morning, people."

And "toughish" it certainly was. By the time the counselors called a halt for lunch, you could describe the Borborygmi in a single word: "pooped." "They'd been walking, with only a couple of brief rest stops, for close to five hours. A lot of that time, the kids were too out of breath to complain.

"Great *job*!" Brad told them, playing "good cop," Arby thought. "So, for your reward, double rations for whoever's extra hungry"—Luther's eyes lit up—"and a nice rest hour after.

Anyone who wants to grab a little nap, even, go right ahead. Me 'n' Sophie are gonna jump over to the top of that rise." He pointed up and to their right. "There's an awesome view from there. Anyone who'd like to join us . . . hey, feel free."

Apparently, nobody felt free. Once they'd eaten, all the kids unrolled foam pads, flopped down on them, and for the most part, fell asleep.

Arby was the exception. He did lie down, but almost at once he realized he was having one of "nature's yoo-hoos." So he wandered off into the woods to take a leak.

He'd gone only a little way when he heard . . . something. Maybe a crackling, like footsteps, followed by a muffled growly sound. He froze. A list of words ran through his mind: "deer-bear-wolf-coyote-cougar-RABID PORCUPINE." Whatever it was was screened by a thick grove of evergreens. He waited and heard nothing more. *Maybe it's just a deer,* he thought. *A little deer, like Bambi.*

So, moving very slowly and *extremely* stealthily, he circled to his left until he was in a position (crouched way over) to spy on what, if anything, was there behind that grove of spruces. He held his breath. He'd always had a thing for Bambi.

Well, there *was* something there, all right. Wildlife? In a way. It was a man that Arby saw, a chunky little dude no taller than himself. And he was hugging an old tree, a partly rotted maple.

Arby couldn't see his face at first. What he could see (going from the ground up) were a pair of sturdy leather boots, bare hairy legs, green cargo shorts (with pockets bulging), a green long-sleeved shirt mostly hidden by the big top-loading ruck-sack on his back, and a wide-brimmed canvas hat with the right side of the brim held tight against the crown.

And now it seemed as if the man was talking to the tree.

"Hurro, hurro, hurro!" he seemed to say. Because his mouth was almost in a hole—a hollow opening in the side of the tree that might have been (it seemed to Arby) the front door to a squirrel's abode (or maybe an old owl's)—his voice was muffled and his words not all that clear.

"Hello?" said Arby softly, not sure he should be answering.

The man spun around. He had plump pink cheeks, bright light eyes. Bushy copper-colored sideburns, and an enormous copper-colored handlebar mustache. He looked surprised but not upset.

"Hello, yourself, young man," he said. "You gave me quite a start, creeping up like that. You could have been . . . gosh, almost anyone. So, tell me now: What brings you to this delightfully uninhabited neck of the woods? Me, I more or less belong here. I'm someone by the name of . . . let's see . . ."—he looked down at the official-looking plastic tag that was pinned to one breast pocket—"Sam T. Quincy, district forester, of course, out here looking for . . ." He paused again. "Oh, yes, the Asian long-horned beetle."

"The Asian long-horned beetle?' Arby asked. "That's a new one on me. Should I have heard of it?" Being the Roach Boy, he felt a certain kinship with all members of the insect family.

"Indeed you should have," Quincy said. "The little guy's a killer. Jet-black body just an inch in length, with white spots on its back. Two two-inch-long antennae, hence the 'long-horned' appellation. And if you look real close, the little sucker's feet have got a bluish tinge, even when they aren't cold."

"Wow," said Arby. "That's a pretty weird-looking beetle. What does it kill, anyway?"

"Just forestfuls of trees is all," the forester informed him. "It has a particular hankering for maples but it'll target birches, willows, and also 'specially poplars—yum!—among others in this area. So far, we've found them only down around New York City and Chicago. They mighta hitched a ride on goods flown in from China—although they most probably came by boat. We're trying to wipe 'em out before they spread into real forests."

"But why were you yelling 'hello' into a hollow tree?" the boy wanted to know. "Were you hoping a Beatle would answer you? Maybe sing a little song?" He smiled at his own wit, then worried that the forester would think he was a wise guy.

Apparently, he didn't. Sam T. Quincy laughed. "Oh, Lordy no," he said. "Not Paul or Ringo *or* an Asian long-horned. The Asian long-horned doesn't speak or sing. What its larvae do is bore a lot of dime-size holes in living trees. That's the sign that I've been looking for—and hoping I don't find. Have *you* seen any holes?" Arby shook his head.

"Me neither—and I'm glad," the forester continued. "And as for what you caught me doing . . . well, I'm afraid that I was

up to just some *very* unofficial research, using that old tree."
He nodded at the old sugar maple. "I have this kind of *hobby*,
you could say." He chuckled. "Some people think it's just a
lot of foolishness." He shook his head and looked down at the
ground.

Arby said nothing. He just stood there, waiting. He was
curious about this "hobby," and he'd discovered that shutting
up worked better than a lot of questions when grown-ups got
all secretive. Sometimes, silence made them quite uneasy, and
in order to feel better, they'd begin to dish.

That seemed to be the case with Quincy. *"This,"* he finally
said, pointing at the tree, "is the sort of tree some people—yes,
myself included—believe to be . . ." He paused and raised that
pointing finger. ". . . an Indian talking tree! You see, it was the
habit of some local tribes to leave . . . well, spoken messages in
certain hollow trees." He stroked his mustache, looking up.

"Messages like 'Lonesome Otter, see if white man's thiev-
ing trading post will swap us guns along with shiny trinkets
for our beaver skins,'" he said. "The senders' voices would get
stuck inside the hollow tree and stay there. Maybe they went
all the way down and into the roots. It's more or less the same
principle as with an echo, I guess—except in this case, the
sound lasts a lot longer. Over time, the messages get fainter
and fainter and finally fade out altogether. But people that I
know have found some that they think date back to the French
and Indian War."

Arby thought the forester was pulling his leg, but being a

respectful lad, he didn't give him the old hee-haw. Instead, he asked, "Any luck with this one?"

"Nope," Sam Quincy said. "There doesn't seem to be as much as a *kemo sabe* in this one, I'm sorry to say. But tell me this: You never did say what you're doing wandering around here on the back edge of nowhere."

"Oh, I'm not really 'wandering around,'" the boy said. "I'm on a hike with a bunch of other people from the Back to Basics Center. We stopped for a rest, back there a little ways." He pointed. "I had to go to the bathroom, and I'd just finished when I heard you over here."

"Ahha. I *see*," the forester said. "Interesting. I know of your center, of course. So, how many are there in your bunch?"

"Well, there's six of us kids and two counselors," Arby told him. "But the counselors are off looking at some view right now. And I think the other kids are all asleep."

"Hmm, that's too bad," said Quincy, though he didn't sound at all regretful. "But maybe one or more of them's awake by now. Then I could ask them if *they've* seen any dime-size holes in trees. I wouldn't bother them for more than a minute or two, I promise you."

"Okay," said Arby. And with that, he led the man back to where the kids were all still stretched out on their pads, still sleeping.

"I could wake 'em up," he told the forester.

"Oh, no, no, no," said Sam T. Quincy. "That really isn't necessary. If you didn't see any holes, chances are they didn't either. Don't disturb them; see how beautiful they look? I used to love to watch my own kids sleeping. Even in their teens, they always looked like little angels."

And he tiptoed around the group, smiling down at all the sleeping faces. Arby himself was struck by how sweet and innocent everyone looked, even the obnoxious EC and the irascible Joey, even the much traveled Primo.

"Maybe you'd like to wait for Brad and Sophie," he suggested.

"Oh, no, no, no," said Quincy once again. "I should be on my way. I've got a few thousand more trees to check before I call it a day. It was nice meeting you, young man. But now I must be toddling."

And with a smile and a wave, he turned and left, quickly disappearing in the surrounding woods.

Arby shrugged and went over to his pad, which he'd unrolled right next to Annie's. When he sank down onto it, he gave a little grunt as the muscles in his back and shoulders started to relax.

Annie opened just one eye and looked at him. "You say something, Arb?" she asked, but groggily.

"Not anything important," he replied, and she went back to sleep.

When Brad and Sophie reappeared, still yapping away about the view they'd gotten to see, everyone awakened and told them to shut up. But they insisted it was time to "rise and shine," so finally, grudgingly, the kids stood up, repacked their pads (and Primo), and got ready to resume the hike.

On the way Arby told everyone about his encounter with the district forester and what he'd learned about the dangers posed by the Asian long-horned beetle.

"Gee, I'd really *hate* it if there weren't so many trees for me to walk around and have their branches slap me in the face," EC said sarcastically.

Brad and Sophie said they'd never heard of any Sam T. Quincy.

22.

Trouble at Camp Two

The Borborygmi were in a pretty surly mood by the time they reached Camp Two. The day's hike had definitely been a "longie"—indeed, a "much too longie" in the minds of everyone but Brad and Sophie. When chore assignments were announced—Joey and Luther digging the "comfort stations," EC hauling firewood, Ragweed starting the fire, and Annie and Arby devising shelters—there was a good deal of muttering. Most of it included language forbidden to the students at the Back to Basics Center. Brad and Sophie either didn't hear it or decided to ignore it; they might have even felt a little sorry for the tribe.

None of the chores were done well, though Annie and Arby and Ragweed made three-quarter-hearted efforts. In the end Sophie helped Ragweed with fire starting, and Brad gave EC a hand (once, caressingly, on her rear end, but also energetically with the firewood). The pits that were dug by Joey and Luther were more like dents, in Annie's and Arby's estimation.

That night, for dinner, Ragweed added water to an envelope allegedly containing "Trailside Stew," and the kids were much too tired to refuse it or even dump on it. Brad and Sophie dined on "Shrimp Creole" over saffron rice and smacked their lips with pleasure.

But several hours later, the scores they'd given their shrimp dinner—a 9 and a 9.5, respectively—took quite a hit. Sophie sat up in her sleeping bag, leaned over to her left, and threw up a bunch of it. EC was sleeping right there on her left and so became the first of the females (other than Sophie) to learn there'd been some virulent bacteria (salmonella, more than likely) in the counselors' evening meal.

Only a very tiny segment of the world's population have been thrown up on in the middle of the night, so it's hard to say if EC's reaction was "typical" or not. It began with the sort of scream of shocked surprise appropriate to being hit on one's sleeping head by a couple of cupfuls of warm gumbo. Then, as consciousness returned—and with it, an awareness of just what sort of gumbo it was that had hit her—EC started to yell words. First came an invocation to the Deity and then, one after another, a couple of vulgar monosyllables, repeated over and over as she leaped up from her sleeping bag and stumbled out the open side of the shelter, followed by a retching Sophie. And pretty quickly, by Ragweed and Annie as well, both hollering, "Ee-*yew*!"

The campfire had burned down to a few coals and there was no moon that night, so it was virtually dark outside. Annie soon realized the boys' shelter had also been evacuated, which meant that, for quite a while, all six Borborygmi, the unafflicted kids, were out there in the vicinity of the two shelters in just T-shirts and underpants chattering and bumping into one another as they tried to locate their backpacks and look in them for flashlights.

Whenever someone ran into EC, there were louder exclamations, followed by expressions of revulsion. Apparently, Brad had managed to exit the boys' shelter before beginning to give up his evening meal.

After a time it became clear that Brad and Sophie were ensconced in their respective "comfort stations." Sound carried well in those quiet woods, and so the kids were soon aware that both of their counselors were *multiply* afflicted. In addition to nausea and vomiting, salmonella victims may suffer—and usually do suffer—abdominal cramping and diarrhea; Brad and Sophie did, and they couldn't help but say so, verbally and otherwise.

EC had finally headed for their water source, a nearby brook, and the remaining five kids, now fully dressed, voiced various reactions to their leaders' plight. There were a few expressions of sympathy (of the "Poor bastards!" variety) and some of amusement, but pretty quickly Joey got the tribe's attention.

"This is our chance!" he exclaimed, not loudly, but with great urgency. "They'll both be weak as kittens. Luther, get the knife. We'll tie 'em up with the ropes from the shelters. Quick, let's get a move on! We'll do Brad first: hands behind his back and feet together, right? And then the same for her. Once we've got them taken care of, then we can relax and make our plan."

It was amazingly easy. Joey was right: Both counselors were very weak and too sick and miserable to put up much of a struggle. The fact that their pants were down around their ankles when the group took hold of them affected their mobility still further. Joey wanted to gag them too, but Ragweed vetoed that idea.

"No way," she said. "Not until they stop puking. We all agreed we weren't gonna kill them."

In the course of subduing the pair, Joey waved Luther's knife around, but he didn't have to put it close to anybody's throat. Luther turned out to be an ace at tying knots ("Got me a merit badge in *this*," he said with a giggle), and Ragweed made sensible suggestions about just how, and how tightly, Brad's and Sophie's wrists and ankles should be bound. Annie and Arby lent a hand in lots of ways, including holding flashlights and later helping to lug the two counselors (their trousers still at half-mast) back to the campfire area. There, they nursed those few remaining coals back into flame. EC returned from the brook when all that had been done, and she had much to say about what she'd gone through and what, if it was up to her, they'd do to Sophie.

Sophie and Brad—weakened though they were (and helpless and embarrassed)—made a few hoarse-voiced statements that they wanted on the record. They told the kids they'd "never get away with this" and alleged that what they'd done amounted to "assault with a deadly weapon." This, they said, wasn't just against the center's rules, it was a *crime*, one for which they could—and would—be sent to jail. But because the counselors were both so sick, their voices lacked authority, and the threats they made seemed almost laughable.

"Yeah, tell me all about it, mothuh," Joey said to Brad.

A little later on, when the kids emptied out Brad's backpack, there at the very bottom, wrapped in a clean I'M WITH STUPID T-shirt, was a handgun, a .38 special.

"See?" cried Joey. "There's your proof. They *were* going to kill us. I'm taking this as evidence, in case we ever need it. Don't anybody touch it. I'm sure his prints are all over the thing." And he rewrapped the pistol carefully and put it in *his* backpack.

Brad tried to offer a rebuttal, insisting that he'd had a gun just for the tribe's protection, in case he'd had to kill a cougar (for example) that had leaped from off a ledge and started mauling someone.

But all that got him was the old hee-haw.

It was still much too dark, all the tribespeople agreed, to even think of heading out, of starting their escape. And they first needed to consult the map Brad had been carrying and see which way to head in order to find a road on which they could hitchhike to freedom. So they sat around the campfire munching PowerBars, waiting for dawn and for the kettle to boil so

they could make some coffee. Everybody was still wired—
"overpowering" the counselors was about as exciting a thing as
any of them had ever done. But they figured they would need
the extra buzz that coffee would provide, given all the sleep
they'd lost and how long and hard they'd hiked the day before.

After some discussion they decided that the smart thing to
do was to tie Brad and Sophie to two trees before they left.

"I say we put them far enough apart so they can't touch,"
said Ragweed with a grin, "but close enough so they can blame
each other for the fix they're in without having to raise their
voices."

"And once we're a long ways away," said Annie, "we can
call up the center and tell somebody where they are, so they
can come and rescue them." She felt that was the right thing
to do—and also that it wouldn't hurt to have said something
like that within Brad and Sophie's hearing, just in case something went wrong and she found herself back at the center,
under their control. The fact that Joey'd said that earlier did
not occur to her.

"Or rescue what's *left* of them," Joey now seemed to enjoy
adding, "if, like, a hungry cougar finds them first. Maybe the
one Brad needed that pistol to protect us from."

"You think that could happen?" Luther asked. "Me, I hope
it won't. I mean, they're assholes—but being eaten by wild
animals? That'd be disgusting, man."

"Look," said Sophie, still in a weak "I could be sick at
any moment" tone of voice. "How about we make a deal?"

Perhaps the realization that she was going to be tied to a tree in hungry-cougar country had just hit her. "Leave us just one thing, besides a little food: that baby ax. We'll swear not to use it—unless we get attacked—until twelve hours after you've gone. Even then, it'll take us a while to cut our ropes with it; it isn't all that sharp. And we won't be in any shape to follow you, even if we wanted to, which we don't. And . . . and when we get back to the center, we won't say anything about you guys attacking us and tying us up. We'll . . . we'll say we got separated. In the dark or something. That what happened was we lost you, and hunted and hunted, and still couldn't find you."

Sophie's "deal" was much too much for EC. "You lying bitch," she said. "You think we're a bunch of *morons*? First you puke on me, and then you lie right to my face like that. I wouldn't trust you if you swore on a stack of Bibles piled up on your mother's grave. I remember what *he* said before"—she tossed her head in Brad's direction—"about getting us put in jail. That's what you'd like to see happen too, and you know it!"

Even Annie had to agree—though not out loud—that anything either Sophie or Brad had to say at this point couldn't be trusted. And that seemed to be what everybody else thought too.

When it was finally light and time to get going, everyone began repacking their backpacks. So of course that was when Annie made the horrible discovery: Primo was missing.

She'd left him in her sleeping bag when she'd leaped out of

it, following Ragweed, who was following the retching Sophie, who was following the befouled EC. She hadn't given him a thought after that, not when everyone was bumping around in the dark, not later when the women's shelter was collapsed so that its ropes could be used as handcuffs and leg shackles, not even in the time they'd sat around the fire, eating and drinking coffee and preparing for the great escape. She'd just known that he was safe in her sleeping bag. Why wouldn't he be?

But now, when she went to get him (him and her sleeping bag, both) and he wasn't there in it . . . well, she went a little crazy.

"Hey!" she cried. "Hey, everybody! Listen up! Who's got my doll? Someone took him out of my sleeping bag. Very funny, ha-ha, but the joke's over. Let's have him back, right *now*!"

People stopped what they were doing. The tone of Annie's voice had that effect. She didn't sound hysterical, exactly. But she was speaking—make that "yelling"—from the heart.

"What?" That was Arby. He came right over to her. "You sure he isn't here? He must be. Maybe under something." He started picking up the folded tarps, looking under them, between their folds. When that yielded nothing, he walked a little way into the surrounding woods.

"Ooh, what a pity!" That was EC, her voice sweetened by phony sincerity. "Poor 'ittle baby gone bye-bye? Maybe wun away fwum mean old mommy?"

Annie looked at her with loathing. She'd be the prime suspect, except she hadn't been anywhere near that sleeping bag for the longest time. She'd been far away, down by the brook, washing vomit out of her hair. And since then, she hadn't been out of Annie's sight.

It also wasn't the time for her to go off on someone. All she could think about was Primo, that she didn't know where he was, that she hadn't taken proper care of him. That this was, basically, her fault.

"Look, I'm not kidding around," she said next. "I really want that doll back." It was making her sick to call him "that doll," but she didn't know what else to say. "One of you must have him. Why don't you cut the crap and hand him over so we can pack up and get going?"

People looked at one another, almost expectantly, Arby thought. But nobody produced Primo and nobody spoke until Ragweed turned and said, "Annie, look. I haven't got your doll, and I don't know where it is. Come here, look in my pack. I swear I don't know anything about this."

Her saying that got everybody moving, bending over, picking up their packs and either emptying them on the ground or showing their insides to Annie, proving that they didn't have the doll.

"I've got Sophie's sleeping bag, seeing as she puked on mine" was EC's statement. "But that's the only thing I have of anybody else's. *See?*"

Annie couldn't believe what was happening. Her feelings of guilt grew into panic. So nobody *had* Primo. What did that mean? That somebody had—what?—*done* something to or with him? Maybe thrown him far into the woods? But wouldn't he have yelled if that had happened? Not necessarily. Maybe he couldn't Could he have been knocked unconscious? Was that possible? Might someone have stomped on him or clubbed him? And then *buried* him? All that under cover of the dark, before they'd gotten the flashlights out?

The only thing worse than that would be that someone had flat-out *killed* him—for no good reason whatsoever.

She ran into the woods, Arby trailing after her.

"Primo?" she called softly. "Primo?" She was crying.

She and Arby stayed in sight of each other, searching and softy calling Primo's name. All they saw were rocks and trees and rotting logs and underbrush; nowhere was the ground disturbed, as if dug into. They covered all the ground within throwing distance of the campsite.

And everyone was ready—chomping at the bit, in fact—to go.

23.

Decisions, Decisions

In times past, Annie had often thought that teenagers like herself had more and harder decisions to make than older people—and than little kids, of course. Little kids lived in an almost decision-free zone; everything was decided for them by adults. And older people, they seemed pretty certain about everything. As far as she could see, they seldom experienced the torment of having to choose between opposite courses of action, each of which, in its own way, had definite attractions.

But teenagers were constantly involved with serious and weighty either-ors. How should she dress: stylish or funky? Exactly like the "in" group or with "individuality"? Should she smoke, drink, and have sex? Was there a safe and happy middle ground between being a sanctimonious prude and a slut? And what about the future? Was it important to work your butt off and get into a "good" college, so as to be eligible for a "good" job that'd make you self-sufficient? Or should you have a good time while you were still being supported by your parents—

and able to enjoy it—and count on charm and friends (and a "good" marriage) to make you happy and successful?

And now, here in this forest wilderness, she was faced with another doozy. Should she leave this place from which Pantagruel Primo, Esquire, had mysteriously disappeared—Primo, her friend and benefactor, who'd probably saved her from incineration? Should she take off with the others and "escape" from what amounted to her second unfair imprisonment? Or should she stay and keep on hunting for her friend?

"I guess we ought to go," she said to Arby, wanting to hear what he would say to that.

She'd offered that alternative because he was part of her problem. If she seemed to want to stay, he probably would feel he ought to stay with her; that was the way he was. And it'd be really unfair to mess with his big chance to escape. He wouldn't even be here, she reminded herself, if he wasn't such a good friend.

"Well," he said, wrinkling his brow, "it's a toughie." His big Adam's apple went up and down, and his large eyes narrowed. "It seems as if *someone* in the tribe must know what happened to Primo. So I'd kind of hate to lose touch with them. And I think it'd be pretty crummy hanging around out here with Brad and Sophie while they're tied to trees. But I guess we could search some more—even more intensively and over a wider area—and then try to catch up with the others. Primo could have been knocked out or something, and I'd totally hate it if he came to and started yelling and I wasn't here to help him."

His saying that confirmed Annie's guess that he was ready and willing to stay if she decided to. Primo hadn't saved *his* life, but he'd decided Primo was his friend too, and he would do his best to help him. That was typical of Arby, of course. But Annie also knew that he would go—go with the others—if she decided to.

She took a deep breath.

"We have to go," she said. "I think we've done our best to find him here. And you're right: One of the other kids has to know something. Maybe if we stay with them and keep talking about him . . ." She shook her head. Arby'd been her loyal friend forever, so she had to give his welfare top priority. But this was another case in which there wasn't an obvious "good" decision, a "right" decision, just waiting to be made. No matter what they did, she knew she'd worry, once again, that the hard choice she'd decided on was wrong.

The other tribespeople had consulted Brad's map and had seen there was a numbered highway that they'd reach by walking in a more or less southwesterly direction. It turned out that Luther's merit badge in knots was not his only one. He could also use a compass, and the counselors had two of them. He helped himself to Brad's.

Joey, Luther, Ragweed, and EC seemed invigorated by having a new goal, by knowing they were heading for a place *they* (rather than Brad and Sophie) wanted to get to. Annie and Arby kept up with the pace set by the other four, caught in the current of excitement and only a bit more conscious of how tired they were. The group was now hiking through hilly, wooded country that hadn't been logged in some time, so it was Luther's compass, basically, that assured them they were headed in the right direction. The map, which showed the ups and downs they covered, as well as the brooks they sometimes crossed and sometimes followed, served to confirm the compass's opinions.

They stopped around midday to eat and rest. It was believed they'd reach the road before it got too dark to see where they were going.

Shortly after they'd begun to walk again, the hikers saw and heard—both in the same split second—the biggest animal they'd come across since they'd set out three days before. But even to the most observant in the group, it was unidentifiable, a flash of brown that, screened by shrubby underbrush, leaped up and off and disappeared, making very little sound once it was out of sight.

"Jesus, what was that?" asked Ragweed.

"Probably a deer," suggested Luther. "I think this is a big deer-hunting scene."

"I bet it was a goddamned cougar," Joey said. "Going by how fast it was—and quiet."

"Did anybody really get a look at it?" asked Annie. "Did it have a tail you could see?"

"I just heard it go," said Arby, "and by the time I looked, nothing. It was a lot bigger than a rabbit or a squirrel, that's all *I* know."

"I'm almost positive it was a cougar, man," said Joey. "The way it took off and disappeared. I'm just glad it went the other way from where we're going."

"I hope it goes and eats that Sophie," EC said.

It really wasn't EC's comment that pushed concern for Brad and Sophie to the front of Annie's mind. Ever since their stop, she'd played hostess to a big stew of things she couldn't keep herself from thinking about—related things, it seemed to her. And Brad and Sophie's present state—helpless, tied to trees— was definitely an ingredient in that stew.

The thoughts had begun with an old familiar one, with Annie asking herself, again, a question about herself: Had she, in the weeks since she'd met Pantagruel Primo, Esquire, become more of an *individual*, more able to stand on her own two feet and be at peace with who she was, or not? Was it possible that she was *still* the same old Annie, the good little girl that her parents wanted her to be?

It seemed to her that she still was—and couldn't stop being—the "responsible" kid she'd been as far back as she could remember. But now maybe there was a difference. Maybe now she was being responsible to things other than her parents' expectations. Starting from the moment she'd met Primo and decided not to tell her parents about him, her life had changed. She'd submitted a story she thought was good and hadn't apologized for it. She'd gone through a trial and a stay in jail—and now some more time with these Back to Basics people—without turning into a compliant wimp and sucking up to anybody.

The ironic thing (she now could see) was that what had helped her a lot in the weeks since she'd met Primo was her parents' insistence on structure and discipline in the life she'd lived with them! Because she was used to doing what *they* told her to do, without complaint, she was much, much better able to do what *she* told herself to do, efficiently and (also) without complaint.

So, at this point, she was both different, surely, *and* (in certain ways) the same.

Now, because she was (still) "responsible," her feet began to drag. She already had the burden of having "lost" Primo, of not having taken good enough care of him—and of not having been able to find him. But on top of that was layered this Brad and Sophie business. Leaving the two of them helpless, tied to trees . . . that simply wasn't her.

Yet she had done—was doing—just that. With every step, she got a little more uncomfortable, imagining a *family* of cougars now, inching forward on their bellies, long tails twitching with excitement, eyes fixed on their next God-knows-how-many meals, sitting there tied up as neatly as the boned and tender roasts prepared by Jean-Batiste, the Sachses' four-star chef.

When the tribe made its next rest stop at midafternoon, Annie flopped down next to Arby, who was sitting with his knees drawn up and his head down, a little removed from the other four.

"Arb," she said, "I'm really, *really* sorry, and I may be being stupid, but I—"

"Yeah, I know," he told her, lifting up his head and interrupting. "You're worried about Brad and Sophie, and you can't stand to leave them like that. I can't either. And it's impossible to know what's best for us *or* Primo. Let's tell the others that we're heading back."

24

Unexpected Happenings

"What? Go back? You gotta be kidding me." That was Joey's stupefied reaction to Annie's announcement that she and Arby were going to return to their previous campsite and make sure Brad and Sophie were okay.

"You think you can find the way?" asked the practical Ragweed. "I sure as hell couldn't."

Annie had been worried about that. "We're going to try" was all she could think to say.

"Me, I don't have anything against Brad and Sophie personally," said Luther. He did that thing with his hair, mashing his bangs down on his forehead. "I think she's kind of pretty. What I don't get is why they do what they do. When I stop being one, I'm not going to have anything to do with kids. Kids are mostly fuckups, just like Joey said. Take it from a man who is one."

"You think she's *pretty*?" EC asked him. "You got peculiar tastes, you know that? I bet she's older than Madonna, even."

"I'll tell you something," Luther said to her with a grin.

"*You* looked pretty when you got back from the brook with your shirt all wet like that. You got nice hooters, honey. You wanna be my girlfriend when we're out of this?" And he leered at her. It was hard to tell if he was kidding.

"Get outta here! You're crazy!" EC dismissed him with a wave, while Annie and Arby collected their share of the matches, food, and utensils that the tribe had liberated from the campsite.

When they were about to leave, Luther held out his knife to them. "Here," he said. "You guys better take the 'dangerous weapon.' You may need it more'n we will. Just don't end up in jail." And he guffawed.

Ragweed gave them a parting hug. "There's moments when I want to go with you," she said. "But then my survival instinct kicks in." She touched the front of her uniform. "I'm afraid I'd die if I dressed like this a day longer than I had to. Good luck, though—really. And say hi to Brad and Sophie. If you find them, that is." And she laughed as if that last part was a joke.

But Annie thought she meant it.

At first, it wasn't too difficult, going in the right direction. They tried very hard not to go in circles. But in less than an hour confusion started creeping in. They realized they were looking at everything *backward*—that what they were seeing when they looked straight ahead was completely unfamiliar because it had been *behind* them before. So they kept turning around and trying to remember if this was the way the woods had looked when they were following the compass's directions. Their route involved more uphills than before, but that made sense: Before, there'd been a lot of going down.

Both Annie and Arby avoided saying the word "lost." "We're probably still going right," Arby said as the sun started to sink. "But maybe it'd be smart to stop and camp right here. This looks like a good spot. And we can get an early start in the morning, when we're fresh. I mean, we always knew we wouldn't be able to get there before dark."

Annie agreed. She had known when they started that Brad and Sophie would have to survive one night on their own, still tied to trees. That wouldn't be pleasant, but it shouldn't prove fatal. And it'd make them all the gladder to be "rescued." She tried to put cougars, wolves, and psychopathic escaped murderers out of her mind.

Arby was right about the spot. It was a good one, under some big spruces and right beside a brook. Annie didn't remember this exact place, but she thought the brook looked familiar.

They made a fire and added boiling water to an entrée labeled CHICKEN AND RICE. After they ate that, they both had a PowerBar. It started getting darker, and they unrolled their pads and sleeping bags.

"You want to sleep together?" Arby asked suddenly. "We could open up both our sleeping bags and have one under and one on top of us."

"Sure," said Annie. "That'd be good." She liked the idea of their sleeping together, now that it was just the two of them.

They got their bedding arranged just right, took off their boots, and slipped under the cover. It was dusky still, not really dark.

This was the first time they'd been alone in a while and the first time they'd ever been together in what might be called a "bed." Annie thought that it was right and proper that the first time she got in bed with a boy it was with her closest friend—a boy she really did "love." She thought this called for some sort of celebration, maybe involving a kiss. They'd kissed before, but only kind of goofily, more or less kidding around—and never in such loaded circumstances.

She rolled over to be facing him and found he must have had the same idea: As her head moved toward him here came his face, and he was smiling, she could see, just as happily as she was.

Their arms went around each other, and their lips came together gently. That felt good, successful, right; and it made them want to go a little farther, make a stronger statement, be more intimate and trusting. To that end, they let their mouths come open and their tongues adventure out and meet, which both of them found thrilling and exactly what the situation called for: slippery secret touches, with saliva.

Annie began to think that, seeing how great the kissing was, maybe they should go on farther still. After all, this was (she told herself) a *very* special situation. For one thing, it was absolutely just the two of them, with no one else around for miles and miles. When was that going to happen again? Maybe not for a long, long time. And for another thing, they were presently in danger, maybe lost. It *could* be that they'd never find their way out of these woods. That was *extremely* special, right there. If they didn't do some things she'd never done before, right now—or at least *start* to do some things—maybe they never would, would never have the chance.

And finally—this was beside the point, but still—it was awfully hot, dressed the way they were, under that thick cover.

"Arb?" She'd taken her wet mouth away from his. "Want to take our clothes off?"

He seemed to need to think that over. "You *want* to?" he asked after digesting her question for a moment or two.

"Sure," she said.

And that brought "Me too!" right away from him.

So they did, not looking directly at each other as they undressed, both standing up, outside the cover of the sleeping bag. But as soon as they'd scooted back down and covered up again, they got their arms around each other right away, both of them excited to be feeling skin, bare skin, and not their own.

In addition to feeling excited—or maybe this was simply part of the excitement—Annie at first felt terribly grown up. This was the sort of thing that *women* did, and she was doing it, taking pleasure in it, conscious of her body in a different way, aware of Arby's body's strong appreciation of the moment and of herself.

Layered on this feeling, though, were other ones: that what they'd done so far was definitely, for her, a long leap forward and that in spite of having made that leap, she was still a kid.

What were Arby's expectations now, she wondered? She knew she'd have to be a lot surer that this was the last day of her life before she'd opt for having sex—even with this boy she thought she loved—especially unprotected sex.

She decided that even if it did real damage to the moment, she'd better ask a question. They'd talked about birth control in general before, but never about how it applied to them, as a couple, specifically. Now, if she got the answer she expected, that'd take care of everything.

"You don't have a condom with you, do you, Arb?" she croaked.

"Well, as a rule," he started, in a put-on, cool-daddy tone of voice, "I take half a dozen on an overnight camping trip. But this time I just plumb forgot." And then he laughed and sounded like the real Roach Boy. "No, of course I don't. And, yes, I know what that means."

He may have sounded how he actually was: more relieved than disappointed.

Annie put her lips on his again. He *was* the best. Now they could go ahead and just enjoy, be total kids, knowing what the limits were, agreed on them. She relaxed—her *mind* relaxed, that is. The rest of her got busy having fun, more fun: experiencing, learning—teaching, too. Initially, excitement put exhaustion on hold, but after time passed, satisfyingly . . .

They never decided to stop, but in a while they did. And then they fell asleep, both awestruck by their own daring—and extremely happy.

• • •

They were up before the sun, still a bit self-conscious when they stood up to put their clothes on, but with little smiles in place. They were anxious to get going. Part of that anxiety was rooted in their concern for Brad and Sophie, but another part had to do with their own situation: Were they lost or not?

Even after walking for a couple of hours, they weren't positive. There were moments when Annie was dead sure that they were lost. But then they'd come to a place where one (or both) of them would look around and say, "*This* looks familiar." They both had in their minds roughly how long in time they'd walked with the group the day before, and that made them think they shouldn't be "there" yet. Neither of them looked forward to the moment (if it came) when they'd have to admit they *should* have gotten "there" by then. Because *then* they'd be admitting that they were really lost.

Before that happened, Annie, leading, stopped dead in her tracks. She put a finger to her lips; she thought she might be hearing things. Arby came up next to her and listened too.

"That can't be the wind," he said more softly than was necessary. "It's music."

Annie nodded. It was surely music, coming from a little way ahead of them, but not a tune she'd ever heard before, and played on an instrument she wasn't sure she could identify. It sounded a bit like a recorder, or a flute, or perhaps a clarinet, very high and pure and clear. The notes followed one another rapidly—drippingly, almost. Like water music.

"D'you think it's Brad or Sophie doing that?" asked Arby. "Sounds like a piccolo, I think. But I didn't see one in their packs."

Annie shook her head. "I don't think it's them," she said. "That doesn't sound like them." She knew that was a silly thing to say, but Arby nodded, seeming to understand.

"But at least it's *someone*," he said. "And they're probably not lost. Maybe they can help us—get us headed in the right direction. I mean, in case we're not." They both were staring straight ahead, in the direction of the music, but all they could see were trees and more trees.

"Sure," said Annie. "Maybe they have maps." And then she thought of psychopathic escaped murderers again. "But let's go really quietly and try to see them before they see us."

"I think we're near the top of a hill," Arby said, moving sideways a little and craning his neck. "It sounds as if the music's coming from below."

So they went on very slowly and soon saw that he was right, that the ground was starting to slope away from them. They could hear the music more distinctly then. It was certainly a happy tune that came floating up the hill.

They stopped behind a big old sugar maple, crouched down, and peered around its weathered trunk. "Oh, wow," said Annie in a whisper.

At the bottom of a moderately steep slope there was a brook. Beside the brook there was a campfire, now burned down to coals, inside a ring of stones. A big blackened teakettle, with steam coming out of its spout, was cuddled up against the coals. On one of the stones surrounding the coals there sat a stack of earthenware bowls, with spoons inside the top bowl in the stack. Beside the bowls, on the next stone, was a paper plate held down by a sizable brown rock that was shaped like the top half of a sphere.

But the main cause of Annie's "wow" was the man who danced—you *could* say "capered"—around the campfire while making music on an instrument she knew is called a "panpipe" and which she'd only seen in a mythology book before. It consisted of a row of hollow pipes of different, graduated lengths that could be blown on (much the way kids blow on the tops of bottles sometimes) to produce as many notes as there are pipes. From it came those lovely, happy, liquid sounds that they'd been hearing.

The man himself struck Annie as being almost as unusual-looking as his instrument. He was wearing a green long-sleeved shirt and green cargo shorts (their pockets bulging) and a sort of campaign hat with the brim on one side turned up and attached to the crown. He had an enormous copper-colored handlebar mustache and bushy sideburns, similarly colored.

"My gosh, it's Sam T. Quincy," Arby said. "I bet you he can tell us which way to go."

"Who?" asked Annie, forgetting she had heard the name before.

At that same exact moment the district forester (it was,

indeed, him) concluded both his dance and his musical perfor-
mance, threw his arms up in the air, and shouted, "Soup's on!
Come and get it!"

Then his glance went up the slope and fixed on the two
heads sticking out from behind the maple.

"You're just in time, you kids!" he added, even louder this
time. "Get your little rumble seats down here!"

25

Reconnecting

Annie and Arby did as Quincy told them to: They went on down. And when they'd gone only partway, his round red face lit up.

"Why, I remember you, young fella-me-lad," he said. "You caught me in the act of looking for a 'talking tree.' And . . . hmm, let's see—I think I recognize the lady with you too. Except she looked a little different—more angelic—with her eyes closed." He winked at Arby. "But I don't believe you ever tossed me any names."

"I'm Nemo Skank, sir," Arby said, sticking out a hand for the district forester to shake, just as his mother'd said he always ought to do when introducing himself to an adult. "But I'd rather you just call me 'Arby.' And this is Annie Ireland."

"Arby and Annie Ireland," Quincy repeated dramatically. He sounded like a circus ringmaster announcing a couple of featured aerialists. "Well, it's a gen-u-wine pleasure to see you both again. So, tell me this, you sharp-eyed little beauties: Any

Asian long-horned beetle sightings since I saw you last?"

"I'm afraid not," said Arby, speaking for them both. "Or I *should* say, I'm *glad* not, I guess. Though, to tell you the truth, we haven't looked real hard for them—or for their holes."

"That's understandable, young sir!" the forester exclaimed. "There's so much that's fun to look at in the woods. And when you're with a gaggle of your friends, all chattering away, you're apt to be distracted anyway. How come there's just the two of you here now? Where's the other angels? Fast asleep again, nearby?"

"Um, no," said Arby. "Actually, they're not. For the moment Annie and I are by ourselves. It's kind of a long story."

"Well, why not park your carcasses and have yourself some eats?" suggested Quincy. "That way, you'll have the time and strength to tell a tale of any length." He nodded in the direction of his campfire. "Grab a couple of bowls; I'll break the bread."

Annie doubted that she'd get much "strength" from Mr. Quincy's "eats." She'd spotted his teakettle from the top of the hill. Maybe he had (in his capacious pockets) instant coffee, or some tea bags, or even (whoopee!) Lipton onion soup mix that they could put in their bowls and pour boiling water over. And if there was bread, it had to be hidden in his knapsack. Probably a loaf of supermarket white—but still, she smiled politely.

And when she bent over to pick up a bowl for herself, all of a sudden she inhaled . . . deliciousness, times two.

It came, first of all, from the loaf of freshly baked bread (it had to be freshly baked, smelling like it did) that had suddenly appeared in Quincy's hands and now was being broken into good-size hunks. It was a fat round loaf that she'd mistaken for a stone (how *could* she have?) from up above.

And then there was the heavenly aroma that came wafting out of the teakettle's wide spout, a souplike, stewlike scent that made her mouth start watering.

Quincy put bread in Annie's bowl, and Arby's, and his own, then lifted up the kettle (using hook-shaped sticks) and poured from it. Out came (plop-plop-plopping) a thick soup (or possibly thin stew), reddish brown in color and full of bits of meat and vegetables. Combined with the dark bread, it made for one of the best-looking bowlfuls of food either of the kids had ever seen.

And it *was* delicious! "Oudadisworl! Fantashic!" mumbled Annie and Arby with their mouths full. The district forester only smiled benignly.

"I hope we aren't eating someone else's lunch," Annie thought to say when she came up for air, looking at the unused bowls. "Are you with some other foresters?"

"Oh, no, no, no," cried Quincy most emphatically. "I'm solo me-o!" he sang out. "A cat who walks by himself, lacking human companionship. But I have a lot of bowls because . . . well, because you never know who might show up, out here in the woods. Why, I believe that if I stayed long enough in this one spot, all my oldest friends would happen by, eventually. But tell me now where *your* friends are and how come you chanced to come upon me."

Annie and Arby looked at each other. Both wondered what—how much—to tell the man. Perhaps his friendliness—and his good hot soup—had an effect. Or perhaps they simply realized, simultaneously, that if they were going to ask for his help, they ought to level with him. In any case, they nodded together in silent agreement, and Arby began to tell him . . . almost everything.

"It's a long story," he said again, "and I hope you'll keep it to yourself. Our parents sent us to this Back to Basics Center because . . ."

When he began to get out of breath, Annie took over, and they went back and forth like that until Quincy had heard the entire truth about their pasts (back home), the center's philosophy and programs, the makeup of the Borborygmi, the overpowering of Brad and Sophie, and the reasons they'd decided to go back to where they'd left the counselors, rather than "escape."

Neither of them mentioned Pantagruel Primo, Esquire, by name, nor did they describe his physical appearance. But they did refer to him. "One member of the group—our best friend, in fact," said Annie, "just disappeared during the last night we were all together. We've been hoping that he's . . . just lost or something and that we'll find him . . . *somewhere*, maybe back there at the campsite. If you could possibly show us how to get to it, that is."

"I can and will do that with the greatest of pleasure," said Sam T. Quincy, "if you're talking about the place where your whole group camped two nights ago. Being the district forester, I try to keep track of every party's whereabouts in this here forest, so when you got moving after your mid-day snoozes, I followed you to where you spent the night. Once I saw you'd settled down, I went about my business. I've been thinking you were in another forest district by now."

He shook his head. "No, your old campsite," he went on, "is not that far from here, maybe . . . oh, ten minutes as the crow flies—that's if the old caw-caw knows some tasty carrion awaits him. On foot, however, it should take us closer to an hour, seeing as we've eaten first."

With that, the three of them wiped their bowls clean with scraps of bread and soon were ready to start off.

"I'll leave the washing up till I get back," Quincy announced in his hearty master-of-ceremonies voice, "and the kettle near the coals, in case some dear old friend comes by."

After a brisk fifty-minute tramp through the woods, led by the pudgy but sure footed forester, the kids heard voices up ahead.

Everybody stopped and listened.

"Sue their asses off" were the first words they could make out. It was Brad's voice, hoarse but unmistakable. Annie thought he sounded desperate, verging on hysterical.

Sophie seemed a lot less certain and emphatic, as usual. "Providing you live long enough to call a lawyer," she said glumly.

"Well, he will and so will you, as sure as toads have stools,"

Sam Quincy hollered to them cheerfully. "Thanks to these fine young 'uns."

And the three of them strode into the campsite and contemplated Brad and Sophie, both still tied securely to their trees.

The counselors were no longer actively sick, but it was very clear they had been; they neither looked nor smelled that great. They looked like people who'd been without food or drink or insect repellent (or a shower or clean clothes) for more than twenty-four hours. They looked like people who'd been struggling, who were helpless and bedraggled.

Brad, however, still had bile to share.

"Fine young 'uns? Those two little bastards?" he croaked through dry cracked lips when he caught sight of Annie and Arby. He addressed the district forester. "Listen here, whoever you are: You cut us loose and then help us take these ropes and tie *them* up. They're members of a tr— . . . a *gang* that jumped on us when we were sick . . . and stole our stuff . . . and tied us to these trees." He was so mad, he was almost crying. "You hear me? I'm going to charge them with assault and . . . and, oh yeah, reckless endangerment. Thank God you caught them, buddy. You got a cell phone on you? I want to call the center—and the cops."

Brad was panting when he finished saying all that. He looked nothing like the Cool Hand Luke who'd snowed her parents, Annie thought. He looked like a raving lunatic who smelled of puke.

While Brad was making his plea to the forester, Annie and

Arby had gone over and freed Sophie, using Luther's knife.

"Hope you're okay," they said to her. "We're really sorry we couldn't get back sooner." They borrowed Quincy's canteen and poured her a cup of water.

"I'm a whole lot better now," she said, rubbing her chafed wrists. She didn't look at them. *She's not the quickest greyhound in the kennel,* Annie thought, *and she's having trouble deciding whether to get mad or to thank us.*

"I don't keep a cell phone in my duffel," Quincy was telling Brad. "I got no need of one." He was inspecting the ropes that went from the tightly bound Brad to the tree.

"Boy," he said, "whoever tied those knots sure knows his onions!" He pulled a big horn-handled clasp knife out of one of his cargo pockets and started sawing away on Brad's bindings.

"And you couldn't be more wrong about these kids," he went on. "I didn't catch them; they found *me*. And they begged me to guide 'em here so they could save your hides. I'm not about to tie them up, and neither are you, young fella. I'm the district forester"—he touched his name tag—"and what I say here goes." He retrieved his canteen and handed Brad his cup of water.

Brad looked as if all that was more than he could process.

"Wha'?" he grunted. "You got no *phone*? They *wanted* to come back? But how come *you* knew where we were?"

"That's my business," said the forester. "I'm *meant* to know who's camping where. But I'd been figgering you and your group had moved along, continued on your hike. I might have come by here again, just to make sure you didn't leave a mess, but I might not have, too. No, if it wasn't for these two kids, you and your fair lady might have found your next-to-final resting place in some old buzzards' bellies."

"I'm not going to lie to you," Arby added. "Escaping from the center didn't sound like a terrible idea to me. But Annie and I wouldn't have been able to live with ourselves if anything bad had happened to you two." He thought that might have sounded a little too real-live-action-heroish, but this was not the time for excessive modesty.

Brad and Sophie looked at each other. Then Sophie sighed and spoke. "This forester guy is right. They may have saved our lives. The truth is that we owe them plenty."

Brad made a face. He clearly didn't like the way this deal was playing out. All this wasn't *his* fault; he had to have a target for his blame.

"You know who I'm absolutely going to sue, for plenty?" he said then. "Whatever asshole company made that shrimp Creole we ate. You ever had food poisoning?" he asked the forester. "I felt like I was going to die, I kid you not. That's how come those little feebs could tie us up like that. We were too damn sick to lift a finger, just about."

He wanted the forester to understand exactly how it was—and see him as the unfairly stricken stud that he believed himself to be.

While Brad and Sophie made their statements and stood

up and walked around the campsite, bending and stretching, Arby started a fire and Annie went and got water from the brook. Pretty soon, Brad and Sophie were enjoying the first food they'd had in a day and a half and cautioning each other about eating too much, too fast. Annie thought it was amazing how quickly they regained their assertive, self-important "counselor" personalities.

Sam T. Quincy finally cleared his throat and said to them, "So, anyway, what's next? You planning to head back to that center of yours, you and your two lifesavers?"

"I guess," said Brad. "Old Smithers—our director—is going to be pissed about those four missing kids. But he ought to understand that isn't *our* fault."

Quincy raised a finger. "He also ought to be *delighted*," he said, "by how Annie and Arby behaved. How they've responded to your program."

Sophie's usual vacant expression lightened. "You know, you're *right*," she said. "We ought to get a lot of credit for . . . well, for having gotten them to shape up so quickly. Most kids don't come around that fast, if ever."

Annie and Arby exchanged looks. *Brad* and *Sophie* were going to get most of the credit for what they'd done? How could Quincy suggest such a thing?

But now the forester was asking a question. "So, when kids *do* improve, do they get—oh, what's the phrase?—time off for good behavior?"

Aha, thought Annie. *The old coot is trying to help us.*

"Sometimes," said Brad. "That's up to Dr. Smithers. He makes all the big decisions. He goes on and on about kids' 'psychological profiles.'" He shook his head. "Usually sounds like a buncha bullshit to me."

"So he's a psychologist, is he?" said Quincy. "Very interesting." And he stood up. "Well, now I must be on my way. Maybe I'll drop by the center in a few days' time. I'd like to show the people there some slides of the Asian long-horned beetle."

"Um, sure—okay," said Sophie unenthusiastically. "We should get going too."

"Yeah—and thanks for helping Arby and Annie be all that they can be," added Brad, with a sarcastic snigger. "Maybe they'll want to go right into the army when we're done with them."

Annie assumed that he was kidding, but it was hard to tell, with stupid Brad. The only thing she wanted, desperately, was the reward that Quincy had brought up: "time off for good behavior."

26

Unravelings

Before they left that campsite, Annie and Arby searched the woods around it one more time—pretending that they preferred to pee elsewhere, given the condition of the comfort stations there. They were hoping, but also in a way *not* hoping, to find an explanation for Primo's disappearance. As long as they knew nothing, they could believe he was all right, somewhere. Once again, their search was fruitless.

It took two days for the four of them to make it back to the center. The counselors knew which way to go in general, but now, lacking their map, they strayed off into unfamiliar territory from time to time and had to retrace their steps in order to get back on track.

Annie and Arby recognized a few places along the way—like the campsite where "they'd" dug those elegant comfort stations—but for the most part, they were delighted to have Brad and Sophie lead the way.

The counselors didn't have a lot of spring in their steps, particularly on the first day; clearly, fasting and an enforced immobility had had an effect on their strong bodies. But their little brains continued to work at full speed. Annie was quite sure they were putting their heads together as they hiked along and would come up with a story that would "work" for them. The first night on the trail, in fact, they began to try that story out on their two charges.

"Just out of curiosity," said Sophie when the four of them were eating that night, "whose poison was it?"

"Poison?" Arby said. "What poison?"

"The stuff you all slipped in our food to make us sick, of course," said Brad. "We're not exactly idiots, you know. You could have killed us with that stuff. In fact, we're thinking that people in less good shape than Soph and me probably *would* have croaked."

"No one put any poison in your food," said Annie. "You got food poisoning. Probably from that shrimp you ate. Just like you told the forester, remember?"

Brad waved a hand. "I made that up for his benefit," he said. "We wouldn't want any outsiders thinking we have kids at the center who are capable of poisoning people. Don't you see? If something like that got around, it'd be real bad for the program. The neighbors might get nervous." And he giggled.

"We can understand you might not want to say who did it," Sophie told them. "Especially if it was one of you. I mean, you *did* come back. Could that have been because you started feeling guilty? We're not saying it *was* you, but we can't rule that out completely."

"Either way," said Brad, "we're glad you did come back, whatever your reasons were. It's still a fact that you were *thinking* you could save our lives, and that's *something*."

The counselors insisted that all four of them sleep in the same shelter, so Annie and Arby didn't get a chance to talk about this newly minted "poison theory" until they were on the trail again the next day.

"I think that's called 'revisionist history,'" said A-student Arby, "and because the kids who are sent to the Back to Basics Center are all supposedly fuckups, like Joey said, it'd be a cinch to blame them—or I might as well say 'us'—for anything."

"Yeah," said Annie, "and maybe Brad and Sophie would rather blame the dangerous kids they have to deal with than admit it's their own stupid fault for bringing along special meals for themselves. No, I bet the poison theory will be part of the official version of what happened, as reported to Smithers. And it probably won't be the only lie they try to sell him."

She proved to be a good prophet. That night they heard the next chapter of the counselors' evolving report.

"You know, as a favor to you, we've decided to soft-pedal our getting tied to those trees," Sophie said. "Your records will look a whole lot better if they don't include any mention of that happening."

"And the fact of the matter is," Brad added, "that it was the effect of the poison, rather than our being tied up, that made it impossible for us to keep you all from taking off—or from chasing after you once you did. Being tied up was only a temporary inconvenience, really. We could have gotten loose even if you hadn't come back, you know. Once the poison was out of our systems, we wouldn't have stayed tied up for very long."

Arby shook his head. "I don't know about that," he said. "The forester seemed to think Luther did a pretty good job on those knots. And it sure took us a while to cut Sophie free."

Brad snorted. "What the forester didn't notice—and I guess you didn't either—were the pieces of shale I was sitting on; that's the kind of sharp-edged stone the Indians used for cutting and scraping. I was just about ready to start sawing on my ropes when you showed up. Like I said before, we're glad you guys arrived when you did, but if you hadn't, we wouldn't have *died* or anything."

"We know you *thought* you were doing us a big favor," Sophie said, "and we'll make sure Dr. Smithers knows what your *intentions* were. We're going to tell him you're okay, no matter what you might have done back home."

"Look," said Annie wearily, "we never *did* do anything bad back home. It was all a big misunderstanding. We didn't—"

"Uh-uh-uh, none of that," Brad interrupted. "We don't talk about the past up here, remember?"

"All Doc Smithers will be interested in is how—or *if*—you've changed since you came to the center," Sophie told them. "Like whether your PHDs have gotten healthier."

"Wait. Our PHDs?" said Arby. "I can't remember what those are."

"Your priorities, habits, and decision making," Brad told

him. "We'll try to make you look good on those in our report to him. And we assume you'll do the same for us, if you get the chance."

"It wouldn't hurt if you told him what creeps those other four kids are," added Sophie. "Maybe you could have overheard them talking about wanting to get us."

Annie or Arby might have nodded then. Not to mean *Oh, sure,* I will *say that,* but more like *Yeah, I see how you want this to work.*

When they got back to the center, the four of them lugged their stuff straight over to the Fresh Start Inn. Shortly after that they joined the rest of the community in the dining hall for lunch. It was obvious by the end of the meal that the Borborygmi and its missing members were the talk of the campus. The buzz of conversation was louder than usual, and a lot of heads were turned in their direction.

After the meal Brad and Sophie said they were off to meet with Dr. Smithers. They instructed Annie and Arby to just "hang out" that afternoon. By the end of the day they'd be told if they'd be added to another tribe or what.

Annie and Arby stayed in the cabin for a while. They decided they would have to see Dr. Smithers as soon as possible. They wanted him to hear their version of their . . . evolution, to see that they were candidates for early graduation, that they *deserved* time off for good behavior. For the first time since they'd gotten to the center, they were hopeful they'd be leaving it real soon.

In less than an hour they got restless and had to leave the cabin. Assuming Brad and Sophie still had the doctor tied up, they wandered over to the athletic field, where a coed basketball game on the asphalt court was just coming to an end. When the other kids caught sight of them, they became the center of a curious, opinionated mob.

"Is it true you fed your counselors *rat* poison?" asked a wide-eyed girl. "Where'd you get it, anyway? I heard they'd both be dead by now it they hadn't known how to boil up an antidote out of roots and berries."

"*I* heard the counselors caught up with the four other kids from your tribe and cut their throats with machetes," said another kid excitedly. "And that you guys had to dig their graves and bury them."

"That's such bullshit," Annie told them. "None of that happened. Whoever told you that is crazy."

"Well, if you had a chance to make a clean getaway and didn't take it, you're the ones who're crazy," a tall boy insisted. "My guess is that the other four wouldn't let you come with them. That's the only explanation that makes any sense."

"Look," said Arby. "You want to know what really happened? In the first place, nobody pois—"

"All right, break it up." The four counselors in charge of the basketball players had joined the group. "Citizenship class starts in two minutes," one of them said, "and I'm wearing the watch. Anybody late gets five black marks, so better move your fannies, people."

Letting out a collective and resentful groan, all the other kids took off, jogging toward the big main building where the classrooms were.

Annie and Arby followed at a slower pace. They decided they might as well check to see if Brad and Sophie were still in the doctor's office; they remembered they could see right into it from the hall. And he'd said his door was always open, hadn't he?

It turned out their timing was impeccable. Dr. Smithers was not only alone in his office, he was also just hanging up the telephone. When he looked up and saw them standing there, he seemed delighted. Wiggling his pointer finger, he told them, "Come!"

When they were seated in two of the chairs facing his desk, Smithers raised his bushy eyebrows and said, "Well, well, well!"

Because he said nothing more but kept that cheerful questioning expression on his face, Annie thought two things: One, *He doesn't have the slightest idea who we are;* and two, *I'd better fill the silence.*

"Nemo Skank and Annie Ireland reporting back, sir," she said. "We're fine. And we learned a lot on that hike, even if it did end badly, in a way. As you know, we had some tough *decisions* to make, but as I'm sure Brad and Sophie told you, we made all the right ones—don't you agree?"

"Ah, yes," said the doctor, but not that emphatically. Some clarity had come into his eyes; he seemed to know whom he was talking to now. "You decided that your proper place was with your counselors, with Brad and . . . so on. Quite correctly, I would say."

"That was our *priority*," said Arby pointedly. "We had a responsibility to our team—our tribe. The kids who ran away were just avoiding responsibility. They didn't want to face their own problems and deal with them."

Smither's face darkened as he nodded. "Indeed, you can't outrun your problems, young man," he said. "As I believe President Nixon put it: 'You can run, but you can't hide.' You can lead a horse to water, but you can't make it . . ."—his eyes went up and away—". . . a different color."

"We've gotten into the *habit*," Annie said, "of preferring lots of *structure* in our lives and respecting people in authority. The *disciplined* individual gets things done; with *too* much freedom, it's easier to lose focus and start to goof off."

After she said that last part, Annie was startled to realize it was something she'd always kind of believed—maybe even something she'd gotten from her parents—and not just a little something that'd help their cause with Dr. Smithers and make them better candidates for some T.O.F.G.B.—time off for good behavior.

"I see," said Smithers. But he looked at them as if he didn't, really, as if he wasn't buying. "You talk a good game, both of you. You're trying to suggest to me that, since you've been here, both of you have added value faster than a dot-com back in '99 to 2000."

"Right, we absolutely have," said Arby. As in their first meeting, whenever Smithers made any sort of reference to money, his voice got deep and juicy, and he seemed a lot more focused. *Well,* thought Arby, *I can speak the language of the markets too.*

"Our little start-up, AnnieArby, Incorporated, has turned a corner," he proclaimed. "We're really bullish about our prospects."

"Is that so?" said Smithers sharply. "I'm not so sure that I agree. And how about *my* business and the way that you've affected *it*? Your tribe, the Borborygmi, has experienced a catastrophic loss: Sixty-seven percent of its assets disappeared four days ago. Do you realize what that means to me? For every day those four kids are away, I lose four days' tuition. At two hundred fifty dollars per kid, that's a thousand bucks a day. *You* helped to make that happen, buster. On top of that, when you poisoned two of my highly compensated employees, you botched the job! Having survived, they still collect their monster salaries. I don't dare lay them off; those missing kids might reappear at any time. So, merrily my expenses roll along, even as my income plummets." He shook his head and made a horsey snorting sound.

"Hold on," said Annie. She was flabbergasted. Smithers would rather have had Brad and Sophie *killed,* so he could save a few dollars? She'd been pretty sure the Back to Basics Center was a *for*-profit outfit (unlike all well-known private schools), but this level of greed was downright gagworthy. "We never poisoned any——," she started.

"What kind of message would it send to this community"——

the doctor didn't even seem to notice she had spoken—"if I were now to have no stern reaction to your actions, if I were just to shrug 'em off, saying, 'Thus the cookie crumbles while the market tumbles'? That would be a message lacking in . . ."—his eyes narrowed— ". . . redeeming social value, I would say."

He sat up a little straighter and went on. "Indeed, the lack of any prompt, decisive move by me could plunge this place into a deep depression. No, the best—the only—thing to do," he said, "is for the two of you to have a little . . . whatcha-callit? . . . a little change of program for a while."

"A change of program?" Annie said. That didn't sound too awful, given what the regular program was. "Like us joining another tribe? Brad and Sophie said that that might be a pos-sibility, although we were actually hoping you'd see you ought to give us some time—"

"Not another tribe, exactly," said Dr. Smithers, interrupting her again. "No, I think the best recourse—for all God's chil-dren—is to have you spend a little time in the ACLU."

"What?" said Arby. "You want us to join the American Civil Liberties Union?" He couldn't have been more surprised if Smithers had told him he'd won the Nobel Peace Prize or been drafted by the New York Knicks.

Smithers had started chuckling. Then full blown laughter bubbled out of him. He shook his head and laughed until a tear ran down his cheek and a thread of drool escaped one corner of his mouth.

"Oh me, oh my," he panted, once he was capable of speech. He wiped his mouth with the back of his hand. "Not *that* ACLU. *Our* ACLU is short for . . . oh, let's see. . . ." He scratched one side of his head, then brightened. "Oh, yes: the 'Auto-Cathartic Learning Unit.' From time to time, we put selected students in it. There, they practice the therapeutic process of . . . what did I just say? . . . auto-catharsis, yes. While in the unit, you will have the opportunity to . . . well, *discharge* the feelings that you have that may inhibit your full appreciation of, and involvement in, our program."

Arby wasn't sure he liked the sound of that. But at least it didn't seem they'd have to go on hikes. And he believed that he and Annie hadn't yet met anyone on campus whom they couldn't manage to outwit. He figured they could feed whoever was in charge of them a line of crap that they'd eat up and even ask for more.

So, instead of making a face, he merely said, "We'll have a cabin to ourselves? Us and Brad and Sophie? But I don't think I saw one with that name on it."

"No, no, of course you didn't," Smithers said. "The unit's in my very own abode, part and parcel of my residence, and a very up-to-date facility. Mrs. Smithers and myself will be your counselors and keepers there, in lieu of bumble-bellied Brad and what's-her-name."

And with that, the director sprang to his feet.

"Time's a-wasting, my young friends," he said. "Ticktock, ticktock, ticktock. Come with me right now. It's later than you think already, kiddos."

27.

In the ACLU

When the director of the Back to Basics Center and his two charges arrived at his bungalow, they were greeted by the woman who the kids had just assumed was Mrs. Smithers, the cigarette-smoking Elton John admirer, Dolores. This day, she had on white capris, silver sandals with four-inch heels, and a pink T-shirt with the words DON'T LET THE SUN GO DOWN ON ME printed on it in black.

"Hi, kids," she said when they walked in the door. "I understand you're gonna hang with us until . . ."—she shrugged—". . . whenever." She kept one hand behind her back, as if to hide a present that she had for them.

"Rooms all ready? Beds turned down?" the doctor asked her.

"Betcha life," she said.

"Then let us toddle down directly," Smithers said.

"Down" was unexpected. Neither kid had imagined staying below ground, in a basement, but Smithers opened a door right opposite the front door, flicked on a light, and with a wave, suggested they go first, down a narrow staircase.

The stairs ended in a hallway with small cellar windows at each end of it. Its floor was brown linoleum tiles over something solid, like cement. There were three closed doors across the hall and two more flanking the stairs.

"The room straight ahead and the next one down," Dolores said.

"Right you are," agreed the doctor cheerfully. "Let's have the boy in here." He turned the handle on the center door and opened it.

At home Arby had heard descriptions (by his uncle) of the "Hole," the generic name for any of the solitary confinement disciplinary cells that exist in most U.S. penitentiaries. And so he recognized the "Hole" right there in front of him.

What he was looking at was a small windowless room with the same linoleum tile floor as the hall and cement block walls painted pink. It was just big enough to contain a built-in silver metal toilet (no seat, but a roll of toilet paper on the floor beside it), a built-in silver metal basin with one faucet, and a built-in silver metal bunk (with thin mattress, ditto pillow, ditto flannel blanket, invitingly turned down), period. There was a recessed ceiling light and a peephole in the heavy door. A couple of sturdy gratings, each about four inches by a foot, covered vents that circulated air inside the cell. There was no handle on the inside of the door.

Arby was horrified. They were putting him in *there*? And

putting *Annie* in another one just like it? He couldn't stand for that; Annie'd become a whole lot more than just a "friend" to him. And "they," he realized, were just an old baldy and a woman wearing hookerish high heels. He could handle them. He was a growing boy who'd gone to all his phys ed classes and had free weights from Sears at home. He wasn't going to let this happen.

So, feeling full of piss and vinegar (as his uncle would have said), he spun around and threw a shoulder into Dr. Smithers's chest. Smithers staggered back. Taken by surprise, he shouted, "Holy Hannah!"

But the Dolores woman kept her cool. She stepped off the bottom step and held out the hand that she'd been holding behind her back. In it was a sizable something that turned out to be a battery-powered stun gun, the kind that can send an electric current coursing through a person when held against any part of his or her body. It did not discriminate on the basis of age, race, or sex, and it was effective through as much as a solid inch of clothing.

The name of this one was in big white letters on its side: THE STUNSTER.

People who've never been zapped by a stun gun can't imagine its effects very well. Cops who are going to carry one sometimes have to be convinced of its potency and volunteer to have one used on them. When they get up off the floor, weak all over and not about to suggest a second test, they're apt to shake their heads and, painting on a smile, say, "Wow."

Arby didn't say anything. He just collapsed on the hard linoleum, trying to understand what had happened. It wasn't pain
he'd felt, exactly, or a shock, just total weariness and weakness.
It was awful. If Annie hadn't come over and knelt down next to
him and put an arm around his head and shoulders, he would
have tried to curl up in a ball.

"Drag him in there," the woman ordered Annie, pointing
at the cell with her weapon. Annie did so, hurriedly. Actually,
she helped Arby to his feet and onto the bunk. "I'm okay. I'm
okay," he kept saying to her then.

"Now come on out," Dolores told her, and she opened the
door to the next cell down. It was identical to the first. "Now
get in there."

Annie did and the door shut behind her. She touched it. It
was sheathed in metal and fit tightly in its frame. She couldn't
hear a sound from out there in the hall and realized she could
yell and scream and cry for help as much as she wanted, and
nobody would hear.

After a while things started happening in both their cells, but
in certain ways, that first, uneventful "while" was the worst for
both of them.

For one thing, there was the getting used to having no idea
whatever of the time. Since coming to the center, they never
had had watches, radios, TVs, or phones, but they'd known
if it was day or night and when today gave way to tomorrow.
They could tell about when they should be eating breakfast,

and lunch, and dinner, by looking at the sun. But in these cells the ceiling light stayed on, and although time passed, no one brought them anything to eat.

There was nothing to read or look at or do once they'd carefully examined everything in the cell. (The toilet paper felt like Charmin, Annie thought.) They both discovered that the faucet supplied only cold water and turned off automatically after it had run for a slow count of five and that the toilet flushed itself, but not very often. Later, Annie tried to count the seconds between flushes, but she gave up somewhere in the two thousands.

After what seemed like a very long time Arby lay down on his bunk and started to pretend he was doing his Roach Boy routine. He thought maybe it was a good thing that he was used to lying still while awake for four hours at a time, making up "what-if's" to think about. He quickly came up with *What if I had, in the hollowed-out heel of my shoe, enough* plastique *to blow my door and Annie's off their hinges?* and *What if, after we got rescued by some guys who were friends of a friend of Uncle Nick's, I was able to sneak into that Judge Rowland's private chambers with the Stunster?* But his old standby *What if Cameron Diaz and I were shipwrecked on a desert island?* didn't seem to work at all in this setting.

When he thought four hours were up, and he was getting hungry, an unwelcome *What if they're going to starve us to death?* popped into his mind. Arby realized he was much more scared of the Smitherses than he'd been of Brad and Sophie.

Annie, for her part, decided not to lie down until she was tired enough to go to sleep. She was determined not to cry or "discharge" any other feelings, in case the Smitherses had some way of overhearing what was going on in the cells, which she considered very likely. She knew they could *see* what she was doing by looking in the peephole. She wondered if maybe it contained some kind of miniature TV camera, so the prisoners could be observed from the comfort of the Smitherses' living room. She really didn't like the idea of the doctor watching her go to the bathroom.

At first, she tried walking back and forth in her cell, but because it was only four pretty short steps each way, that got old fast. She then got down on the floor and did a few push-ups and sit-ups until she decided that was a stupid idea. Even if she did a million push-ups and sit-ups, she wouldn't be strong enough to stand up to The Stunster.

She wished Primo was there and smiled when she remembered his vegetation-in-the-toilets trick at the county jail. *If only he were here now,* she thought. She tried to figure out what could possibly have happened to him, but she stopped when she almost started to cry.

Sitting on her bunk, she admitted to herself that she was afraid. And hungry. Maybe the Smitherses were going to let her starve to death. Her and Arby both. . . . *Dear Arby.* Maybe they'd then tell their parents they'd wandered off on one of their hikes and disappeared, lost in the wilderness. She knew that, at some point, she was simply going to have to pee.

• • •

The first thing that happened, after that initial "while," was the light in the cells went out. In the pitch dark both Annie and Arby assumed that they were being told it was night and that they should try to go to sleep. Annie felt her way over to the toilet and started to pee; almost at once, the light came back on. When she'd finished and was back on her bed, miserable and lying turned to face the wall, the light went off again.

Arby sighed when the light went off that second time and muttered to himself, "They're messing with our minds."

Both kids fell asleep and were awakened by the light coming on again; it seemed brighter than before. Both thought they'd slept a lot less than a whole night's worth, though they couldn't be sure of that.

Soon after the light came on, Dolores appeared in Arby's cell (the door opened soundlessly) holding in one hand a cardboard bowl that seemed to contain raisin bran and milk with a peeled banana on top and, of course, the Stunster in the other. She put the bowl on the floor while Arby kept his distance, and she left without speaking. Then she repeated that routine in Annie's cell.

In each room the bowl was eyed suspiciously, but after a minute or two curiosity and hunger had their way. First, the banana was picked up and sniffed all over. It smelled okay— like a banana—so a little nibble was taken out of one end, followed after a bit by another, and another, and another, until the whole banana had been eaten, but very slowly.

Annie remembered hearing Cousin Fleur say that by eating slowly and taking small mouthfuls, a person could eat
less—and not gain weight—while feeling full, even though she
really wasn't.

Because there were no spoons in the bowls, they either had
to use their fingers to pick up the cereal or try to slurp it out
of the side of the bowl. Annie used both methods, once again
starting very cautiously and tasting, tasting, tasting (like a little
old lady, she thought), on the lookout for any unusual flavor
that might come from a drug or poison. Arby just sipped and
slurped. He considered raisin bran to be an old persons' cereal;
his uncle Nick went for it. He was more of a Wheaties guy, having moved up from Cap'n Crunch. But he scarfed down that
bran one-two-three and would have happily accepted another
bowlful.

After that breakfast nothing happened until "lunch"
arrived. Annie thought it came a little soon after breakfast,
but she wasn't sure. It was brought by the same armed waitress.
On a little cardboard tray there was a paper cup of skim milk,
an unusual "bowl" made out of bread that held hot tuna cas-
serole, and in one corner, what looked like a little pile of dog
poop. After some moments of indecision both Annie and Arby
snatched the bowl off the tray, and following more cautious
sniffing, they devoured both the bowl and its contents. Afterward, they drank the milk, which was a little watery for their
taste.

When Dolores collected the trays—at the time she came

with their "supper"—she picked up (in both rooms) the "dog poop" and took a bite out of it. "Don't care for chocolate, honey?" she asked sweetly as she shut the door behind her.

The next night, with their bologna sandwiches, she brought cups of "chicken soup." "I couldn't find the soup pot, so I made do with our old bedpan," she informed the kids. "But the soup tastes fine." Both of them passed on the soup (diplomatic Annie flushed it down the toilet), but it did smell good.

For the next day's lunch, what was on their trays *was* dog poop, as Arby soon found out.

By the third "day" both kids were feeling that their sense of time was totally screwed up. Meals were arriving sooner or later than expected, and the light went on and off a lot. They both were sure they never got a full night's sleep. Once, raisin bran arrived when they were both expecting "supper," and when questioned, Dolores simply shrugged.

Without warning, her voice started coming out of one of the gratings. She read them newspaper stories that dated from the first President Bush's administration and also recipes for delicious summer meals.

But to Annie's great annoyance, she mispronounced the name of certain herbs (saying "or-a-GAN-o") and one fancy lettuce ("ara-GOOL-A"). "That's *tyme*, you idiot," Annie suddenly shouted when their keeper gave that herb the "th" sound.

Dolores also read them bits from *Gray's Anatomy* that made them both uneasy:

"The surface of the nipple is dark-colored and surrounded by an areole having a colored tint. In the virgin, the areole is of a delicate rosy hue. . . ."

and

"The testes are suspended in the scrotum by the spermatic cords. As the left spermatic cord is rather longer than the right, the left testicle hangs somewhat lower than its fellow."

What was her *point*? (both kids asked themselves). They started hating the sound of her voice.

As the days (or was it only hours?) passed they both began to get jumpy. Neither of them had ever experienced this level of powerlessness and aloneness.

For the first time, sentences beginning with *If I get out of this alive . . .* began to pop into their heads, and though only Arby had been made to practice praying, they both did some of that, wholeheartedly.

28.

Test; Results

When the light went off at whatever time it was on whatever day it was, Annie and Arby were twitching around on their bunks, doing all there was to do when the light was on. In other words, they were wondering and worrying. The light going off provided a third option, going to sleep, so they both closed their eyes and took a shot at doing that. Even though they'd exercised only their nervous systems, they were both exhausted. So, in a while, they managed to doze off.

When the light came back on, their eyes reopened to (what else?) the horror of their situation. Annie quickly resumed wondering: Was there any chance at all her parents might . . . do *something* (unexpected, brilliant) that would save them?

But when her door swung open, it was Dolores, not her parents, who came in. For whatever reason, she was wearing Louis Vuitton's version of an army uniform: an olive satin military jacket with gold buttons, a khaki nylon skirt, and (incongruously) a pair of ballet slippers, pink ones. This time the plate she brought held fish sticks and spaghetti in tomato sauce.

Annie, lying there, let out a groan. She felt like eating something light, a "breakfast," maybe tea and toast or cereal, not this heavy, smelly stuff. If she got a normal breakfast, then there was at least a chance a normal "day" might follow, one which they'd be let out of there in time to join another tribe for "lunch."

Fish sticks and spaghetti would never be the first meal of a "normal" day.

Arby saw the food and was hit by an overwhelming desire to brush his teeth, a thing he hadn't done for days and days. The inside of his mouth already had the taste of fish sticks—ones that had spent time in a metal garbage can, outdoors on a sunny August day.

"So, today you're going to do a little test," Dolores told the two of them, in turn. "Fish is brain food, and spaghetti's what they eat before a marathon. Don't say I'm not a thoughtful person, giving you a perfect meal like this before your test."

Of course Annie and Arby tried to imagine what kind of test they might be in for. Annie suspected they'd be made to write an essay (groan!) on "Why and How I Was a Bad, Bad Borborygmus." Arby, not the most coordinated kid on the planet, could see them making him walk back and forth on a balance beam over a pit containing . . . (Oh, right, perfect!) snarling pit bulls.

But when the self-styled "thoughtful person" came to get their plates and them a short while later, she had information, too.

"Doc's all excited," she informed them. "Get this: He says this test is doing for the measurement of adolescent rage and overall dangerousness what the Stanford-Binet—whatever *that* is—did for the measurement of intelligence. It's brand-new and gets administered and scored by the man—some eminent psychologist—who made it up. For security reasons, so that it can't be copied or prepared for, no one else is ever allowed to *see* the test, not even school directors like Doc. Ain't that a hoot?" She really *was* excited.

"It's already been given to all the other kids here," she went on, "and nobody did any good at all. What that proves, Doc says, is that they all do need to be here. And he's sure as anything that you do too and that you'll do really awful on the test. Seein' as you've been in the ACLU a while, you *must* be angrier than anyone. You understand what I'm saying?"

Unfortunately (they both thought), they did. They were about to take a test that they'd do badly on, probably get real low failing grades. And their results would be used to "prove" to their parents that they should stay there at the center for a good long time. They'd of course try to do "well" on the damn test, but what were the chances that they—mere kids—could outsmart the brainiac who'd invented the stupid thing? They were, as the saying sometimes goes, "screwed, blued, and tattooed."

Dolores escorted Annie and Arby up the stairs and into the Smitherses' dining room, where they were told to sit in chairs at the opposite ends of the table. Two freshly sharpened number two pencils sat where you'd ordinarily find two forks.

A moment later, Dr. Smithers bustled into the room followed by a short man wearing tan riding breeches, calf-high black leather boots, and a bright red vest over a black-and-white-striped shirt (rather like a football referee's). He had a small head, black patent-leather hair parted in the middle, and a bulbous nose. In his right eye was a monocle.

"Students, let me introduce you to a man who . . ."—Smithers paused—"who needs no introduction. He's the genius we have to thank for this fine test, Professor Roll."

"Thank *you*, Doctor Smithers." Roll made a little bow in the school director's direction. "And now, without further ado, I will pass out the tests."

This he proceeded to do, putting one facedown before each kid.

"All righty," he then said. "Directions, coming up. Please write your name and today's date on the back of your test papers, on the top line, after where it says 'Your name and today's date.' If you're not sure of your name or the date, don't guess; I'll fill them in a little later. On the next line, after where it says 'Examiner,' write in *my* name. And so you don't have to guess at it, I'll give you both my card."

He took a pair of cards out of a vest pocket and put them on top of the overturned test papers.

"Now then, attention!" he continued, not giving the kids time to look at the cards or write in his name. "You are about to take the Postpubescent Pathology Estimator, or the 'PPE,' as we call it for short. There are no 'wrong' answers on this test, although seven out of ten of your answers probably won't be 'right.' Feel free to guess if you're not sure what you think or if you don't feel like thinking. Once you begin, you'll have thirty minutes, more or less, in which to complete the test, but don't turn over your papers and start until I say 'Begin.' Any questions? All right—ready? Go!"

Annie looked at Arby. She was wondering what they should do; the professor hadn't said "Begin," and much of what he *had* said seemed pretty weird to her. Then she remembered that she hadn't put his name on the back of her test yet. So she quickly did that, after checking out his card. It said he was "DeForest Roll, Professor of Behavioral Analysis, University of Iceland (Vatnajökull Campus)."

Arby was looking back at Annie. He must have also noticed that the examiner hadn't said "Begin," because he made quite a show of putting down his pencil, folding his hands, and looking expectantly at Professor Roll. Annie followed suit.

"Oh, all right, you smarty-pants," said Roll. "Begin."

In less than half a minute Annie knew the test was not like any other she had ever taken. The word for it, she thought, was "screwy."

On the first page were some fifty true or false questions. As a rule, the true or false section of a test was Annie's favorite, and for one good reason: It was by far the easiest. There would always be a few answers that you knew for sure. And on all the other questions you have a fifty-fifty chance of being right. If you had a lucky guessing day, you'd ace that section of the test.

But these true or falses were not like any she had ever seen before. How could a person even *guess* if these were true or false?

1. That was no chicken, that was my wife.
2. You gotta dance with who brung ya.
3. A watched pot gathers no moss.
4. *N'entrez bien* le fox away.
5. That was no piccolo, that was my fife.

And so on. . . .

The only one Annie was pretty sure she might have gotten right was:

50. All vegetarians eat vegetables, and some humanitarians eat people.

The multiple-choice questions on the next page were equally confounding. For example:

7. One-legged people stink the worst at:
    (a) hopscotch
    (b) step dancing
    (c) three-legged races
    (d) ass-kicking contests

or

15. Snow shoveling is to heart attacks as marathon running is to:
 (a) great lung capacity
 (b) total boredom
 (c) intergluteal chafing
 (d) carbo loading

or

37. If you are good at math and science, you may be:
 (a) apt to forget your socks
 (b) a successful drug dealer
 (c) in love with your pocket protector
 (d) failing English

But then Annie got to the very last question on the test.

50. Which of the following is the title of an excellent short story?
 (a) "Life Begins at Forty"
 (b) "Life's Darkest Moment?"
 (c) "The Life of Riley"
 (d) "Life on the Mississippi"

She stared at it, rubbing her eyes in disbelief. As she did so she heard a sharp intake of breath from the other end of the table, and she guessed that Arby, too, had just read the fiftieth multiple-choice question.

"Life's Darkest Moment?"? It was the question mark after "Moment" that told her (and him, too) that this was (just had to be) *her* story, the one that had gotten them into all this trouble. But how could it have gotten on this funky test? Where could this Professor Roll have heard of it? Surely not at the University of Iceland (Vatnajökull Campus).

But then, looking at the card again, she focused on his name: DeForest Roll. She said it to herself, but faster: *deforestroll.* And then, just slightly differently: *the forest troll.* Yikes!

At that moment it all added up: his saying "seven out of ten of your answers probably won't be right" (which echoed words she'd heard before: "We will all be good at only three out of every ten things that we try to do"), a test with the initials *PPE,* and now her story's title and "the forest troll." This slightly nutty prof was (had to be!) Pantagruel Primo, Esquire, very much alive and kicking!

With fireworks going off in her head, Annie was *that* close to shouting *Primo!* at the moment she looked up and saw him with a forefinger pressed hard against his lips. Arby was staring at him too and nodding. The other person in the room, Dr. William McGuffey Smithers, was looking out the window. (He was trying to mentally multiply $250 by eighty-six, which was the number of students that would continue to be enrolled at the center, not counting the four who had run off, but counting the two who were about to fail this test. Of course he couldn't multiply by eighty-six in his head, but he *could* do $250 by one hundred—$25,000 a day—which'd be a bit too high, so maybe $150,000 a week would be real close. Even after deducting expenses, that'd be a nice chunk of change for him and the missus, he figured.)

Behind his back, Annie and Arby were looking at each other as if they'd just heard the poet Byron say, *On with the dance! Let joy be unconfined.* . . . Yep, they *were* excited. But a warning look from the "professor" made them wipe those feelings off their faces. Primo (neither of them had a doubt that it was he) was back, in charge, and with a plan well under way. Their job was to shape up and play along.

"All right, kiddies—pencils up!" he told them. "I'll now collect your papers and begin to total up your scores. I'd like to do that right here at the table, if that's okay with you, good doctor," he then said to Smithers. "Perhaps you and your two charges would be kind enough to leave me now, so I can concentrate without distractions. I'll join you in a very little while, I promise you."

Annie and Arby got up and followed Smithers into his cluttered living room, where Dolores was already sitting. There were literally hundreds of gewgaws and knickknacks (ranging from pre-Columbian artifacts to souvenir ashtrays from Myrtle Beach, South Carolina) on all the shelves and tables, and not one piece of the furniture seemed to have been acquired at the same time (or by the same person) as any other piece. The kids perched side by side on a love seat covered in a red, white, and purple flowered chintz, the sort of very large and ugly pattern that Dolores might have gone for in a shirt, thought Annie.

She glanced over at Arby and admired the pathetic "look" he'd managed to come up with. He sat hunched forward, not leaning against the back of the couch, with his head bowed and both hands hanging down between splayed knees. But every so often, he'd make his eyes shoot up, as if he still retained a tiny spark of hopefulness. She decided she'd just go for stoic calm: She crossed both arms and buried her chin in her chest. Neither Smithers nor Dolores said a word to them.

It was a good fifteen minutes before the professor came into the room. He had some rolled-up papers in his hand and a stern look on his face.

"Ah," said Dr. Smithers, smiling, sure of what was coming next. "Any luck, Professor?"

"That depends on what you mean by 'luck,'" said Roll. "As I'm sure you have assumed, my test is made in such a way that luck can play no part in its results: the students' scores. It measures adolescent rage and dangerousness scientifically and accurately. A student can't get 'lucky.' As I explained to you before, scores between 1 and 3.3 describe a youngster with few problems beyond a little normal anxiety. Recipients of scores between 3.4 and 5 should be watched closely but not really apprehensively. Those who score between 5 and 8.5— like all the adolescents I tested here before—are threats to others and to themselves and definitely belong in a well-designed residential program. The few who score between

8.5 and 9.7 or 9.8 need constant supervision; they're likely to explode at any moment."

He took a deep breath, looking extremely serious.

"This pair"—he tossed his head in Annie and Arby's direction—"is at a level that I wasn't sure existed in developed countries. I shall have to handle them with the greatest possible care until I get to show them to my colleagues at the university. The girl came in at .66, the boy at .58. Both less than *1*, my friend. To use a totally unscientific term, these two are 'total pussycats'!"

29

Negotiated Settlement

Dr. Smithers rocked back in his chair.

"They are?" he said. He slapped his forehead: *thwack*! "I can't believe it."

"Well, you better start to," Roll advised him. He was crossing the room toward Smithers, smiling broadly. "I'd say that they provide the perfect justification—were one needed—for your program here, the proof, as it were, of the goodness of your pudding. I congratulate you, sir." He held out his hand, and Smithers, still bewildered, stood and shook it.

"So," continued the professor, "I suppose that your work with them is done and that you'll be pleased to have me take them off your hands. What I will do is reunite them with their parents first and then, with their permission, take the youngsters with me to the university. I can tell you here and now that I have some colleagues who are going to simply *flip* when they stand face-to-face with those two! For years some people have believed—in fact, they have said 'known'—that teens *this* levelheaded, friendly, and cooperative could not possibly exist."

"You're saying you . . . you want to t-take them with you *now*?" Smithers stammered. His mind was racing; this was unbelievable. These kids had been in the ACLU for days. They had to be absolutely *bursting* with anxiety, confusion, and a raging desire for revenge. But on a psychological test that measured all those things—and had shown all the other kids at the center to be overflowing with them—they had come up almost empty! Their results could not be argued with; the unthinkable had happened. The center's program had somehow really worked for these young people—he couldn't imagine why—and there really wasn't any reason for the two of them to stay. Except . . .

Roll had turned away and was chatting easily with the kids. Smithers heard them telling the professor something about ". . . hard but good." And then Dolores was right there beside him, yakking sotto voce in his ear.

The words that made it through the daze that he was in were "stall . . . impossible . . . a charlatan." And most insistently, ". . . five hundred bucks a day!"

He pulled himself together and cleared his throat so loudly that he got Professor Roll's attention.

"I'm afraid that won't be possible," he rasped. "Them leaving with you, I mean. We have a—what?—a *routine*, like a . . . *procedure* they must follow. There's *paperwork* to be . . . er, um, *completed*. And I must telephone their *families*. Invite them up here, *absolutely* . . . for . . . because . . ." He looked down at the rug, then pulled his ear. Would Dolores realize he was sending her a *signal*? Not that they'd ever discussed any signals, but he had heard that women had great intuition.

"Ceremony," she supplied, giving him the *reason* he'd been groping for.

"We have to have," he started up again, "their graduation *ceremony*. Line up a speaker and all that. We couldn't let these youngsters leave our midst without a little . . . let me see . . . oh, my . . . yes, *pageantry*," he blurted out, enormously relieved. "Another week—ten days—with us, *at least*, should do the trick. I know *you* know, Professor, how important *closure* is."

Dolores Smithers, nodding, crooned (but very softly) one of Elton's sweet refrains: "I think it's gonna be a long, long time." Ten days was about the max that they could stall. Five thousand bucks could not be sneezed at.

"What?" said Roll. He adjusted his monocle and peered at Smithers. "Really, Doctor, that's a lot of twaddle. The thing these kids need most right now is O-U-T. They should get back to normal living. Here, there's just too much pathology around; the atmosphere is heavy with dysfunction. It's my professional opinion that they would suffer pain, and possibly real damage, from another week or more on this campus. I must insist I be allowed to take them—"

"Oh, put a sock in it, Professor," Dolores Smithers interrupted. "You heard the doctor, and he's in charge for now. The kids are staying, you are going—game, set, and match. We're the legal guardians of those kids, and all you are is a wandering consultant. Follow the doctor's orders; *sayonara*, baby."

Now it was Professor Roll who had turned to look out the window. He had a disgusted look on his face; it appeared he couldn't stand the sight of either of the Smitherses. He rubbed his bulbous nose and then his thumb and first two fingers together; he might have been drying them—or trying to think of something.

"I hardly can believe my ears," he said as he turned back to face his hosts. "In all my life I've never heard of such a thing; the head of a residential treatment center refusing to discharge a healthy patient—*two* healthy patients, in this case. Believe me, I shall be reporting all of this to the officers of the national association as soon as I am off this campus. As you well know, if they were to cancel your accreditation, this center would become a ghost town; population: two. Clients would avoid it like the plague."

Clearly, that threat hit Smithers pretty hard. The confidently happy face he'd worn when Annie and Arby were taking the PPE was ancient history; now anxiety and confusion reigned. He looked over at his wife. She wasn't any help. Her body language was defiant: head up, chin out, arms folded tight. What was she thinking of? Was she going to challenge the professor to some test of strength or daring, with the youngsters as the prize?

The silence in the room was broken at that moment by loud knocking on the bungalow's front door. Dr. Smithers turned toward it, but before he took a step, Dolores had him by the arm.

"Stay still," she hissed into his ear. "We've gotta make a deal with Professor Big Nose here. Whoever it is will go away if we don't answer."

But a moment later, the knocking started up again, and even louder this time. In addition to the knocking, there was someone yelling something.

"Prize patrol!" was what they heard inside the bungalow. "Prize Patrol for Doctor William Smithers!"

Dolores relaxed her grip. A big smile spread across her face. "I can't effin' believe it! It's the goddamned Prize Patrol," she said, delightedly while heading for the door.

And so it was—or appeared to be, anyway. Through the open door waltzed Sam T. Quincy, the erstwhile district forester, still with plenty of copper-colored facial hair, but now snappily attired in creased flannel slacks, a dark blue blazer with a crest on its breast pocket, and a spiffy patterned ascot round his neck. He was carrying a six-foot-long facsimile bank check made out to William McG. Smithers for the amount of ten million dollars. With him came two comely young women in virtually see-through silk blouses, bearing in their smooth and slender hands a big bouquet of flowers, a bottle of champagne, and a dozen colorful helium-filled balloons. As they came in they did a lot of jumping up and down and squealing.

While Annie and Arby looked on in amazement, Quincy presented Dr. Smithers with a standard-size bank check and then got one of the girls to take a few Polaroids of Smithers and himself holding the ends of the big facsimile check while smiling broadly. Dolores's eyes never left the words written large on it: TEN MILLION DOLLARS. When she had the chance, she went and whispered in her husband's ear.

Had Superman been in the room, his superhearing might have very well picked up the words ". . . don't need the two brats now."

Once Quincy and his assistants left the bungalow and things were back to "normal," Dr. Smithers turned to the professor with a "let's be friends" expression on his face. Apparently, his attitude had changed somewhat.

"I'm afraid I spoke a little hastily before," he said to Roll. "On . . . er, *reflection* I now see that your *prescription* is a wise one. By all means, feel free to . . . shall we say *convey*? . . . These youngsters to . . . wherever. In these unprecedented circumstances, we can surely grant a . . . *dispensation*, yes, from our—that is to say, the *center's*—closing ceremonials."

"All right," said Roll, now playing the good winner, but also quick to take advantage of his victory. "And may I also assume you'll telephone the families *at once*, telling them that both their kids have completed your program with high honors—and in record time—and that tomorrow you'll be mailing them your written recommendations, for them to use as they see fit?"

"Oh, yes," said Dr. Smithers, with dollar signs still dancing in his head. "Yes, happily I'll do all that."

"Well, in that case," said Professor Roll, "as soon as I'm informed you've really done those things, your accreditation will be safe, and those unprofessional and insulting remarks made by you and your wife will be just between the five of us—forgiven, yes, if not forgotten.

"And now," he finished, "we'll be going. You needn't bother showing us the way." He bowed stiffly from the waist, and then, propelling Annie and Arby ahead of him, he sashayed out the door.

"Say nothing till we're in the vehicle," he murmured to the two as they walked away from the bungalow. A big black van with darkened windows was backing up the driveway toward them. On it were distinctive license plates: STQ.

It stopped in front of them; a door slid open. Primo and the kids hopped in.

"*Primo!*" Annie and Arby chorused happily as soon as the door slid shut again.

"You're all right!" she cried. "Thank God!"

"You *saved* us!" Arby added. "You're the greatest!"

And then they both started babbling a bunch of questions: "How? . . . When? . . . Where?" The driver of the van looked on, now smiling broadly. He was, of course, the man the kids had once believed to be the district forester and who the Smitherses had thanked for making them new millionaires.

"Well, let me start by saying I imagine you were quite surprised to see your woodland guide had taken on a new identity," Primo told the joyful pair. "But no more surprised than *I* was when he picked me up the night that Brad and Sophie got so sick. Little did I know there was a small device in that doll's bod, so he could come and find me anytime he decided to cast off the spell and end the little joke he'd played on me."

Annie's mouth fell open. "You mean . . . ," she started.

"Oh, yes," said Primo. "The driver of this vehicle, your forest guide, and the deliverer of bogus bank checks is none other than my dear old friend and sometime rival, STQ—Slurpagar the Quaint!"

30

Epilogue

Annie Ireland and Nemo Skank were welcomed back to Converse High without a problem. Ninety-nine percent of the student body and all but one or two unpopular faculty members had spoken of their incarceration as either "a screwing" (the kids) or "a travesty of justice" (the teachers). Both Annie and Arby let it be known that they'd hated "boarding school" (as they thought it best to call the Back to Basics Center) and had pleaded with their parents to allow them to return to Converse High. That provoked approving nods from everyone.

It hadn't taken Annie and Arby long to realize that Primo had been wise to let their careers at the center play out the way they had, even though they wouldn't have minded missing out on the ACLU. If he'd whisked them off right after Slurpagar found him (during the hike), they wouldn't have been so easily and understandingly welcomed back by their families. It was much better having the kids officially "discharged" (as it were) from the center, rather than just showing up back home with some made-up story explaining why they'd run away, or something.

Annie found that things were delightfully different at home. She didn't know whether to credit Dr. Smithers's recommendation, the long-range effects of her parents' weight loss, or her new improved self-image for the change. Her cousin Fleur told her she wished *she* had a boyfriend half as nice as Annie's.

Arby's mom loved having him back home, and his uncle Nick, after reading the center's recommendation, agreed the boy had gotten all he could (except for maybe a few phone numbers) out of the boarding school experience. The manager of the Fright Factory was overjoyed to learn he wasn't going to lose the "original" Roach Boy. The Roach Boy himself had plans (so far unspoken) to marry Annie Ireland someday.

Postscripts

Luther, Joey, Ragweed, and EC were never caught and are still out there somewhere—maybe, under different names, taking (and cutting) classes at your local high school.

As for Slurpagar the Quaint and Pantagruel Primo, Esquire? Well, before they hugged the kids good-bye, they told them that they thought they'd take a break from playing tricks and making people look like fools. But a few weeks later, when Annie and Arby read a news story about a new casino going up in Las Vegas under what was believed to be "Icelandic owner-ship," they wondered if perhaps their two old friends had decided that, while on their break, it'd be fun to just sit back and watch a bunch of people act like fools without the slightest bit of help from them.